*Glimmers of Light
In A Betraying Land*

# Glimmers of Light
# In A Betraying Land

by
## GIORA PRAFF

Translated from the Hebrew
by Mordecai Schreiber

**Shengold Publishers, Inc.**
**New York**

Many thanks to Heidi Praff
for assisting in the editing of this volume.

ISBN 0-88400-159-8
Library of Congress Catalog Card Number: 92-082824
© Copyright 1992 by Giora Praff

Published by Shengold Publishers, Inc.
18 West 45th Street
New York, NY 10036

Printed in the United States of America

Hannele was bursting with joy. Suddenly everything seemed as rosy as the flowers in her neighbor's garden.

"Mama, who else from Glinyany will be going with me to the boarding school in Lvov?"

Rivka, a heavyset woman with pleasant features, had been busy all morning preparing Hannele's valise. Since the arrival of the Russians, the Hochberg household has enjoyed prosperity. "May the Almighty bless Stalin and the Bolsheviks," she thought. Now she could prepare a different meal for her family each day, and from time to time she would go the Malka, the seamstress, to try on a new dress made from fabric sent to her from America by her brother Yossl.

"Hannele, I'm packing Ziporah's wool coat for you. The nights in Lvov are cold. The wagon should arrive any moment. Hurry up, Nushka is ready."

"Nushka Biller?" Hannele asked.

"Yes," her mother answered, "she will share your room. You cannot ask for a more well-behaved roommate. Go say goodbye to your father."

Aharon Hochberg was in the middle of a lively discussion with Vasily, the Russian officer who lived in their house. Vasily was a short, squat Russian with coal black hair and a pale face. He hated army life and missed his wife and two children back in Stalingrad; he hadn't seen them in three months. He had been a member of the Communist Party since childhood, when he had joined the Komsomol, and he'd never had a heretic thought about socialism. As a supply officer for an armored unit, he had free access to the flour and sugar supply. His presence at the Hochberg home was the reason for their economic recovery and the relative prosperity of the family members. Rivka liked Vasily, a quiet person with a benign smile, who sat on the doorsteps of the house wearing his uniform and played with little Eju.

"Vasily, come taste the dumplings I have prepared," Rivka called out.
Vasily did not respond. He was deep into an argument with Aharon.

"Communism is worse than the czarist regime, not only for Jews and
Zionism. It oppresses every sound creative soul and uses coercion to
destroy the enlightened world," Aharon argued, as he paced the floor
with his walking stick, waving it in the air from time to time.

"Stalin is an insane dictator. Listen to me; his days are numbered,"
Aharon went on.

"Come now," Vasily responded pleasantly, "since I came your lives
have changed. The pantry is always full. Rivka is happy. Hannale is going
to a school in Lvov which is subsidized by Stalin. You can now afford
to give Ziporah a dowry. Your older son Munyu is no longer a bum; he
is helping me with bookkeeping and inventory. And you, after being
operated on in Vienna for a terrible cancer, are getting a free supply of
dressing for your colostomy."

Aharon began to waver. After all, Vasily was right. How could these
hated Bolsheviks have improved life beyond recognition in their house
and in Glinyany in general, he wondered. The village was clean; the men
had to work, no parasitic behavior was allowed, and only a few young
men were drafted by the Red Army. Well, a country had the right to
maintain a strong army, especially when a showdown with Hitler was
quite likely. But they mercilessly suppressed the Zionist movement,
those bastards, and had exiled several of its main activists to Siberia. As
for him, he was "lucky" to have cancer, for it prompted the political
officers to leave him alone, since they assumed that his days were
numbered.

At the same time they forbade any Ukrainian nationalistic activity,
which was good for the Jews. The Ukrainians kept a low profile. They
were never hospitable to their Jewish neighbors, but their children went
to school with them and they played together. The harassment of Jews
which sometimes resulted in death, stopped. The Polish regime had
seemed helpless in the face of Ukrainian nationalistic outbursts, which
had always been accompanied by anti-Semitic violence. But the Bolsheviks were merciless, and the Ukrainian population learned immediately—the hard way—that it had to give up its aspirations for

independence for a while and hide its hatred of the Russians and the Jews.

Aharon continued his internal debate: "Take Vasily, such a friendly man. Can he be a Communist and believe with all his heart in the revolution? No, he is an exception. To hell with Bolshevism and Communism. They are the embodiment of evil. Even the Ukrainians, like the Zionists, have a right to national self-determination."

Vasily had great respect for Aharon, the head of the family, who was fifteen years older and—despite his cancer—always stood tall. He had brown hair and his temples were starting to gray. His eyes were always smiling. His thin mustache was carefully groomed, and a small goatee covered his chin, as was the custom among scholars. Aharon's sense of humor was famous. From every corner of Galicia and Poland, requests came for him to lecture. Al his brothers were learned, and his father was an acclaimed scholar of the Torah. Whenever the name of grandfather Yehezkel was mentioned, people got chills down their spine, and they were filled with reverence. Aharon carried on the tradition with pride. He treated everyone, young and old, rich and poor, with respect. He knew how to listen, and people often sought his advice. He was fluent in Polish, Russian, Ukrainian, German and Yiddish. The gentiles respected him and avoided making anti-Semitic comments in his presence. He was always well dressed, and used a walking stick he had inherited from his father. His manners were Austro-Hungarian, and he spoke with nostalgia about the days of the Hapsburg Empire, where he had lived in his youth. He was a follower of Ahad Ha'am, and spoke perfect Hebrew. As a devoted Zionist, he dreamed of Zion as a spiritual center that would be a light unto the nations. German culture was close to his heart; he felt that the culture of the Slavic people was inferior and he raised his children in this spirit. His oldest daughter Ziporah was married off to Tzvi Meidanek, who was the principal at the school where she taught. Tzvi was perfectly fluent in Hebrew and sang like a nightingale; Aharon's heart swelled with joy whenever he sang in Hebrew. Aharon had talked Ziporah into marrying Tzvi despite the fact that he was paunchy and twenty years her senior. "Here is an ardent Zionist young man who will continue the tradition of the Hochbergs," he would rebuke her. But Ziporah's heart belonged to Anshel Dresner, who was her own age; he was studying medicine in Vienna. Anshel was a thin redhead with a shy smile. He always excelled in his studies. As the first to study medicine, he was the pride of his family. This well-to-do yet warm family had no particular interest in the Jewish national movement. Aharon despised those *nouveau riches* people, devoid of depth and spirituality, and, although he liked Avremele the goldsmith, he wanted his daughter to marry a learned man who was committed to the land of Israel and to Zionism.

"Leave me alone, Papa," Ziporah would wail. "He is a great teacher, an important person, and he sings well. But he is much older than I, and I don't feel attracted to him. Anshel is my age, and his family is so good to me."

Ziporah, at nineteen, was attractive. Her flowing brown hair was often parted into two braids. She was tall, her lips were delicate, and she had her mother's sculpted features and her father's kindness and refinement. She was praised for her looks, her intelligence, and her gift as a teacher.

Rivka empathized with her daughter, but felt sorry for her sick husband. She wanted to please him with all her heart, knowing how deeply he felt about the Zionist dream. She attended to him faithfully during his illness, and after his recovery she would carefully dress the skin around the bag into which he defecated. At times the area would become infected, and the puss-filled sores had to be drained by Doctor Ness, the town's physician. Aharon's fever would rise, and sometimes he hallucinated. Aharon and Rivka were deeply in love, having refused, despite all the protests to be married off through a matchmaker. Rivka had fair hair and gray eyes. Her light complexion belied her Semitic origin. Now her face was often flushed by the heat of the kitchen, and she hardly ever removed her apron. Her family was large, and she was blessed with many sisters. She had met Aharon by accident at a ball in honor of the Jewish soldiers in Emperor Franz Josef's army who had come back to Glinyany after the First World War. It was love at first sight. Despite the absence of the traditional matchmaker, and because of the Hochberg family's social status, her father agreed immediately to give her hand in marriage, and even gave his daughter a modest dowry which included bedding, silverware and towels. Rivka bore Aharon four children. Ziporah was the oldest, followed by Munyu, Hannale, and finally Eju, the baby of the family. She was proud of her family. Everyone sought her advice about daily matters, and her wit became famous. She had a sharp tongue, and did not spare the rod with her children. Eju, her baby, always clung to her skirt. Rivka often pinched Hannale and reprimanded her for her burning jealousy of her little brother. Hannale was convinced her mother completely ignored her. She would sit in her father's lap and enjoyed listening to him read Hebrew poetry and prose. But most of Rivka's care was directed at Munyu. He was eighteen, a slim and pale youth who nonetheless was quite strong. He was quite energetic, and he soon befriended Vasily, and because of his talent for accounting he would help him with the army inventory. Munyu seemed to have found himself, but Rivka suspected that something worrisome would happen.

It was one of those winter nights in Glinyany. The Hochberg family was seated around the large dining room table. Vasily was with them. Suddenly they heard loud Russian voices at the entrance door, ordering them to open up. Aharon hastened to the door, and as he politely greeted his visitors, Vladimir, the usually well-mannered political officer, whom they knew well, burst into the house.

"Where is Munyu?" he hissed. "He must come with me immediately for questioning."

Munyu was at the Zionist Youth Club. It had been converted into a card-playing club after the arrival of the Communists.

"*Gevalt, shma yisrael, gevalt*, what's happened?" Rivka cried, as her alarmed children went to hide behind her.

Vasily was stunned, but he immediately stood up and asked Vladimir what was wrong.

"It has come to my attention that Munyu is dealing in sugar, flour and who knows what else. He is a thief. Lech, the Ukrainian, admitted during his investigation that he had bought goods belonging to the Red Army from him. Be careful, Vasily, you may also be in danger."

Rivka felt the blood leave her face; she made a supreme effort not to pass out. Aharon was livid, and was about to express his feelings towards the Bolsheviks. Rivka jerked her head as if bitten by a snake and looked Vladimir straight in the eyes.

"I'll bring him immediately. It is a disgrace that our son would do such a thing. God bless Stalin and the Red Army."

Hannale and Eju trembled with fear as their mother put on her hat and her heavy coat and rushed to the club. Vladimir was somewhat mollified, and apologized for his outburst. He ordered the armed soldier who accompanied him to leave the house immediately, and started to explain that an investigation had been initiated regarding the disappearance of supplies belonging to the Red Army, and that he was charged with the unpleasant task of bringing in the son of the respectable Hochberg family. The children slowly calmed down. Hannale even smiled at the Politruk, who face broke into a broad smile, revealing his gold teeth; he made an attempt to pinch her on the cheek.

"Sweet Hannale, lucky is the one who will be the first to win you over."

She blushed and ran back to her room. Vladimir and Vasily started to chat, but Aharon was still in a rage. The door opened and in came Rivka, dragging Munyu.

"You thief, you criminal, how could you do such a thing to our family," she shouted in Russian and started beating him with the fireplace shovel.

Vasily tried to protect him, and even Vladimir seemed uncomfortable as he watched this domestic scene. Munyu started to cry and asked for forgiveness.

"Go to your room," his mother told him. She turned to Vladimir and said in softly, "I know what he did is serious. But I cannot turn my son over to the NKVD. Vladimir, you know our family. It would be a tragedy. Please, tell Piotr that if he forgives Munyu he will get two beautiful gold teeth from Dr. Biliger. Please," she started crying. Vasily whispered something to his fellow officer and the two left the house.

"Bastards," Aharon snapped, "they will pay for this. Someday we will have our own country in the land of Israel and we'll make them pay."

"Hush," Rivka told him, alarmed by her own word. She had never before addressed her husband like this. She left the room choked with tears.

Aharon turned to his library. Whenever he felt low he would reread the letters of his friend Asher Korech, who lived in Eretz Yisrael. He loved the Hebrew language, and Asher's letters from Zion made him feel festive and uplifted. He would start daydreaming, imagining himself there, occasionally seeing himself as some biblical hero in a classic scene. He lit his pipe and drew deeply. He did not even notice his children playing nearby, and did not even think of reprimanding Munyu for what he had done. He was lost in his biblical dreams and in the land of Israel, forgetting that he was in the Galician town of Glinyany, on Polish soil.

Hannale's mind reviewed the whole episode as she rode in the wagon to Lvov. Nushka sat beside her, clinging lightly to her. The road seemed interminable.

"Have a safe journey, Hannale," yelled Grisha, the young son of Jan, their Ukrainian farmer neighbor. He waved to her and ran after the wagon for a while. The girls giggled. Grisha was about sixteen, and his blond hair was long and curly. His eyes were small and deep set. He always followed Hannale. "Here, catch," he cried, throwing some apples into the wagon.

Night fell and it grew cold. The girls bundled up in their coats and clung to each other. Nushka fell asleep on Hannale's shoulder, but the latter was too excited to sleep. It was her first trip to Lvov. She had heard about its coffeehouses, theaters, and its beautiful buildings. She had never before been to a real city. She dreamed about all the things she had never seen. She imagined picturesque palaces and gardens, with princes and dukes in all their finery. Once she had seen an automobile in her village, and she was excited over the prospect of riding in one soon. Finally Hannale fell asleep; when she awoke, she saw a marvelous scene. They had reached the outskirts of the city; the sights unfolding before her seemed somehow familiar. She awakened her friend and the two of them gazed at the great metropolis in front of them.

Lvov was indeed a charming city. The architecture was Austro-Hungarian. The years of the Hapsburg empire had left their imprint. There were beautiful gardens and coffeehouses everywhere. Chauffeur-driven automobiles with well-dressed passengers blew their horns. Military personnel walked in the streets, but even the presence of Bolsheviks did not lessen the city's vitality.

The girls' boarding school was located in a wealthy neighborhood.

Inside, it was spotless. Velvet curtains covered the tall windows. The girls were shown to their room by a pleasant Polish woman, about sixty years old, who was dressed as a hotel chambermaid.

"Welcome to our school. We have a long, illustrious tradition of outstanding education." She continued in a whisper, "Since the Communists are here, you will have to learn Marxism and Leninism." She added, "It is my task to look after all your needs while you are here. The spoken language here is Polish, but at certain hours you must speak only Russian. Yiddish is completely forbidden. You must obey all the rules."

The two girls had stopped listening. They turned to their room, which was simply furnished, yet sparkling clean.

Hannale enjoyed school and stopped missing her home. She was a vivacious girl. She did well in school, and was liked by all who knew her. She often took long walks and observed all the wondrous sights of the city. The girls' dormitory was close to the center of the city, and son ardent admirers began to appear, eager to spend money on her.

One day she saw Haim. He had just turned 21, a proud Jew, born in Leningrad. Tall and thin, his brown hair was cut military style and his eyes glistened. His uniform was somewhat unkempt, but he made sure his officer's insignia was clearly visible. Recently graduated from the military academy in Moscow, he was stationed near Lvov with a tank unit which he commanded. Haim was a brilliant officer whose future in the army seemed promising. He would not tolerate any anti-Semitic remarks, and would often find himself in a fight which left the offender badly beaten. Being an exemplary officer, he was spared a court-martial.

It was a spring day. The air was still cool, but pleasant and clear. The sky was deep blue. The sun was shining, but its heat was not felt. A group of Russian soldiers was strolling in the street, a rather common sight. Hannale and Nushka were sitting in a coffeehouse near the school, having a pleasant chat. Suddenly the soldiers turned and came into the coffeehouse. They sat down and started humming a Hasidic song. The girls grew quiet and carefully eyed the soldiers. Their eyes met the soldiers' eyes, and Hannale saw the young, slim officer looking at her curiously. He stopped singing. She looked down, and then up again, and he smiled at her. "Beautiful teeth," Hannale thought. She disliked gold teeth, and was glad his were white and even. Suddenly he said in Yiddish,

"Would you like some ice cream?"

She was so taken aback, that she couldn't speak. Finally she told him in Russian,

"My name is Hannah Hochberg, the daughter of Aharon Hochberg of Glinyany." She realized he hadn't asked for her name, and she stammered in Yiddish,

"Yes, I love ice cream. Can my friend join us?" Before she had finished her question, she was sorry; now this lovely youth might turn his attention to Nushka.

"Of course," Haim laughed. "Now that I know your name and place of origin, I'll introduce myself. My name is Haim Manger, and I am an officer in a tank unit stationed near Lvov."

"Tank? What exactly is a tank?"

Haim laughed, "It's like an armored car which can fire."

"Why do you need such a thing?" Hannale asked.

"We don't believe the Germans will keep their promise, and if we have to, we will fight them with our tanks, guns and airplanes." He made an unsuccessful attempt to explain the nature of those weapons.

"And what are the two stars on your neck?"

"I am an officer," Haim explained, "and this is my rank." This seemed to impress her more than the explanation about the tanks. She finally asked where he was from, and he told her about his family in Leningrad, and about his father, an old Communist who had taken part in the October Revolution. He had learned Yiddish mainly from his grandmother, since his own parents had turned their backs completely on Jewish language and culture. Throughout, he did not take his eyes off her. Noticing her embarrassment, he said,

"Tomorrow I'll take you to the movies."

The two started seeing each other. Hannale began to taste of the rich cultural life of Lvov. Naturally, in her letter home she never mentioned Haim. She was well aware of her father's feelings toward the Bolsheviks.

She always felt comfortable in Haim's company. He showered her with gifts, and she would often receive a bouquet of flowers in her room. The other girls were desperately jealous of her. But Hannale continued to do well in her studies, and even after her teachers found out about her boyfriend and her frequent outings, she was not called into the office, and her schoolmates' anger kept growing.

One day Haim did not arrive at their meeting spot. Hannale went up to her room, and a young, unkempt soldier showed up. He seemed somewhat frightened and his voice shook as he whispered in her ear,

"Captain Manger ordered to take you immediately back home to Glinyany, without delay. Our unit was instructed to move west right away. The high command believes the Germans are about to attack."

The Germans would not dare attack a mighty nation like Russia, Hannale thought, but on the other hand they had dared to invade Poland and were now at war with Great Britain. She felt she was shifting from a dream to reality. Suddenly she remembered her father's last letter, in which he had mentioned that he had gotten a letter from Avremele Sofer in western Poland. Avremele described the harsh plight of the Jews under German occupation. He mentioned crowding them into ghettos, forced labor, and even executions. "It is not possible that a nation that has given rise to Goethe and Schiller would do such a thing," Aharon wrote. "I will not allow the spread of such vicious rumors." Suddenly she was gripped by the awful feeling that some catastrophe was about to take place. She paled, and asked in a weak voice,

"What about my friend Nushka?"

"Pack your things and leave her a note about your sudden departure due to your father's illness."

On the way to Glinyany she noticed the change that was taking place. While Red Army trucks and tanks were moving westward, there were wagons of villagers loaded with their belongings moving in the opposite direction. There were no farmers in the fields, and the sky seemed to be darker than the usual. She saw occasional blue and yellow flags on the rooftops, waving in defiance. The road seemed interminable, and the dust was rising in front of them because of the tracks of the tanks passing by.

When she arrived in Glinyany it seemed nothing had changed. Her mother sat on the doorstep and was amazed to see her daughter get out of a military truck. She ran up to her.

"Mama, the Germans are very likely to attack. The Red Army is ready for battle. Where is papa? I must see him immediately."

"Hannale, what's all the commotion? Who is this soldier, why did you come home?" She continued in a whisper, "You know father's feelings towards Stalin's soldiers."

"There is no time, Mama, we must decide quickly. Where are Eju and Munyu? Did you hear from Ziporah?"

"Your father is speaking at the club, and Munyu is there too. Eju is at Dr. Biliger's. I told you he was studying under him, didn't I? It is a great honor for us. Eju will be a dentist. Ziporah and Anshel went on their honeymoon to the Carpathian mountains, on the Rumanian borders."

"Anshel?" Hannale was stunned. "What about Tzvi?"

"*Oy vey*, Hannale, don't ask. Terrible trouble. Tzvi had a nervous breakdown and had to be hospitalized about two weeks after the wedding. We had no choice but to annul the marriage. The rabbi was most understanding. We didn't want to burden you, Hannale, so we didn't write to you about it. She finally married Anshel, and thank God everything is well."

Hannale turned and walked out, heading for the Zionist Club. She thought she noticed a blue and yellow flag on one of the rooftops. When she passed the house of Zenig Tuss, a municipal official who was one of the leaders of the Ukrainian community of Glinyany, she saw someone familiar in the window. She recognized the face, but could not place this person with the evil grin. Suddenly it came back to her. "It's him!" She started to run towards the club, trying to suppress the thought of the horror stories she had heard about Bogdan Petlura, that Ukrainian nationalist adored by his countrymen and notorious for his bloody pogroms against the Jews. When she reached the club she squeezed among the assembled crowd. At the far end she saw her father standing at the lectern.

"There is no cause for fear," her father was saying. "Panic will only make things worse. We do not know whether Germany will attack, and if it does attack and push the Bolsheviks back to their land, our situation will improve. The Zionist movement will prosper again alongside the national Ukrainian movement."

Suddenly a middle-aged Jew interjected,

"What about all the reports of killings emanating from Warsaw?"

"They must be exaggerated. I repeat, an enlightened nation which has given rise to writers and poets and other great men, to which I belonged in my youth, and which helped cure my cancer, will not engage in wanton killings." He spoke with great self-assurance, and when he finished his speech there was loud applause. Hannale stood there and watched him, and suddenly she felt estranged from him, angered by his words.

"My Hannale," her father whispered, a tear in his eye, when he saw her. "Welcome back from faraway lands, my dove." He laughed, then grew serious and asked, "What brings you home; what are you doing here?"

"I wish I could be as steadfast in my faith as you. Wouldn't we be better off if we packed our belongings and went east? I have seen many families with their belongings going east in their wagons." There was despair in her voice. He tried to respond but she went on. "Papa, don't be angry, but with the help of a young, Jewish, Russian officer whom I met in Lvov, I can transfer our family to a safe place."

"This is unheard of," he fumed, "my daughter fraternizing with Stalin's stooges. We won't leave our place and we won't give up our freedom." He waved his cane in the air and said, "Go home at once and tell your mother I'll be a little late." He turned away and started chatting with Joseph, the tailor. She started to cry. As she sobbed she heard Joseph lowering his voice and saying,

"Aharon Hochberg, I have listened carefully to what you said. I have an important question for you: My daughter Marta is married to a Soviet citizen. My entire family was offered a free passage east. What do you think, should I accept the offer or not? How do you feel about it? I have always listened to your advice, and I am willing to listen now."

"Yosel," Aharon said, "don't let them talk you into leaving. The Communists are the embodiment of evil and the misfortune of the Jewish people. Stay here with your family and help us reestablish the Zionist movement.

"This is what I intended to do," said Joseph, "but I wanted to hear it from you."

Life seemed to go on unchanged. From time to time one could hear the rumble of guns and the bursts of machine guns. In the town one could see more and more yellow and blue flags, and there was a sense of anarchy. Convoys of military vehicles rolled eastward, carrying a growing number of wounded.

The Hochberg household was well supplied, thanks to Vasily, who now had to leave his unit. Hannale and Eju would cling to each other when they heard the cannons, although they were no longer little children.

One day Rivka cried out, "Munyu!" Then there was silence. She held out a letter:

"Papa and Mama, Hannale and Eju: I am writing you these lines after deciding to leave town and join the Red Army. I am sure you, Papa, will forgive me, but I have no hard feelings against our Russian brothers. I don't espouse the Marxist ideology, but I believe with complete faith that I'll be better off with them than under German occupation. I love you all, Munyu."

Aharon remained silent as Rivka cried. He embraced her and tried to calm her down. Hannale wished to emulate Munyu, but deep inside she hoped Haim would come and take her with him. Yanek, the barber, arrived at that moment. His face was bruised from beatings.

"When I left the barbershop on my way home, several Ukrainians stopped me and called me a dirty Jew. They said that they'd settle their account with me when your Bolshevik allies escaped." Some of them wore uniforms and caps marked with yellow and blue. I did not respond, but they beat me and, if not for the fact that a military vehicle was nearby, I might have been in much worse shape."

"Go home in peace," Aharon said reassuringly. "These are feelings of frustration and bitterness on the part of the Ukrainian national movement. They will get over it once the Russians leave."

One morning a young officer arrived at the door of the Hochberg family. He knocked on the door and waited. Aharon was still in his nightgown and cap, and he looked suspiciously at the officer, who seemed exhausted. He was not shaved, and his eyes were shining.

"My name is Haim Manger," he said in Yiddish as he saluted. "You must be evacuated immediately. The Germans are closing in. They are only a few days away from this town."

Aharon was totally surprised. How was it possible for an officer of the Red Army to speak Yiddish? The voice was the voice of Jacob, but the hands were the hands of Esau. Suddenly he flared up and snapped,

"You are the one who met my daughter in Lvov."

"Yes," Haim said, "I love your daughter and I would like to help you all. There is little time." As he spoke he let himself into the house and was about to climb the steps when he saw Hannale standing at the entrance to her room. She had been awakened by the knocking along with the rest of the family. When she saw him she started crying hysterically and said,

"I knew you would come." She ran toward him, about to embrace him, when she noticed her father and stopped.

"Quick, Hannale, pack your things." Turning to Eju, he said, "You too, young man, we must leave in 10 minutes."

"Stay where you are," his father thundered. "And you too," he turned to Hannale, "don't you dare disobey me. No one is leaving with this Bolshevik."

Haim was furious. He looked at Aharon.

"If not for your daughter, I would call you a few names. Don't you understand? The Germans are coming. Rumor has it they liquidate every Jew they see. Do you wish to leave your family's fate in their hands and in the hands of the Ukrainians? Don't you feel the catastrophe approaching?" As he spoke he grasped Eju's hand and pulled him outside. He lifted him and put him on the tank and turned to Hannale. Aharon followed him outside, limping on his cane.

"Come down immediately," he waved with his cane. He took hold of the boy's leg and started pulling him down. Hannale looked on, paralyzed. On the one hand she felt an overwhelming desire to join Haim, realizing the danger they were in, but on the other hand she could not leave her parents, whom she loved dearly. She was unable to move. She couldn't think clearly; it was as if she had become paralyzed. Eju started to cry and climbed the tank again, but his father started beating him with the cane and he ran into the house, looking for his mother, who was also at a loss for what to do.

"Hannale," Haim cried, his despair growing.

"I cannot leave them here by themselves. . . ." Her face was stony. "Go in peace," she added. "I will never forget you."

He looked at her stunned, unable to believe what he saw and heard, realizing he was not going to take her along. Resuming his place inside the tank, he shouted an order, the tank engine roared, and the tracks ground forward, leaving behind a pillar of smoke.

Dark days came to Glinyany. More and more blue and yellow flags were seen on rooftops. Aharon forbade his family to leave the house after dark. Mendele, their neighbor's son, was badly beaten by Ukrainian thugs. The boy became mute. Despite the tranquilizers and pain pills prescribes by Dr. Nass, the boy wouldn't speak a word.

There was no sign of Russian rule. The red flag had been removed from the town hall. Zenig Tuss, Aharon's old acquaintance, who had been a junior official all his life, appointed himself mayor. A Ukrainian militia was organized. Each morning it members were seen marching in the town hall courtyard, dressed in brown uniforms with a blue and yellow band on their sleeves. From time to time they attacked a Jew. Plundering of stores was a daily affair, and Jewish storekeepers were afraid to open. The Hochberg family was fortunate to have enough food. Rivka continued to prepare a different meal each day, but would no longer sit on her doorstep. She couldn't help feeling they had missed their chance. The behavior of the Ukrainians did not surprise her. She knew many of them personally and had good neighborly relations with them. The farmers' wives would solicit her advice and bring her some of their produce. She was very skeptical of Aharon's faith. He would say,

"Here is an example of an oppressed people who need a release for their national feelings."

She sensed the hatred of the radicals, and knew that the slightest provocation would lead to a pogrom. It would only take a small spark to light the fire. She had heard stories from her mother about the behavior of the Ukrainians and felt a sense of doom.

She knew nothing about the Germans. Jews had never had it better than under the enlightened rule of the Hapsburgs. Both she and her husband were enchanted by Austro-Hungarian culture. They raised their children in that culture. They all spoke German well. Despite the rumors about atrocities against Jews in western Poland and Warsaw, she attributed them to the Poles rather than the Germans. But when she read the letter from Gittl, who had lived in Warsaw for years, she felt weak at the knees and started to shiver.

My Dear Rivka,
As I am writing these lines, I feel that the end is near. Since the arrival of the Germans our situation has been deteriorating. First they started with restrictions and prohibitions against the Jewish community. We were made to wear a yellow band, but we were still allowed to go to work and maintain community life. The situation worsened when they decided to put us into a ghetto. The crowding is inhuman, and there is hunger everywhere. Little Ruchele contracted typhus and died. My other children are dying of hunger. We cannot exceed the rations allocated to the ghetto by the Germans, and anyone who tries to smuggle food into the ghetto is shot. My husband, Eisen, lost his mind, and has been hallucinating. He looks like a skeleton. There are bodies lying in the streets, and the stench of death is everywhere. The ghetto police, under German orders, arrests people every day and send them to unknown destinations. No one has come back, and rumor has it they are being executed. I cannot go on. If not for my two children, I would put an end to my life. Run for your life as long as you can. When you get this letter I may no longer be alive.

The letter was brought by an eighteen-year-old named Gershon. He had managed to escape from the ghetto because of his Aryan features, and was able to travel without being stopped. It took him three weeks to reach Glinyany from Warsaw. He was looking for a safe haven, and was bitterly disappointed to find out that the Russians had disappeared. He was unfamiliar with the Ukrainians, but immediately felt their hostility. He ate his fill for the first time in months.

Rivka cried disconsolately, "If I had only known, Gittl, you poor soul, I would have brought you here."

"I don't intend to go through this again," Gershon muttered. "Tomorrow at dawn I'm heading east. German convoys are only days away from here. If the choice is between Hitler and Stalin, I assure you, Rivka, I would choose the latter."

Rivka did not respond. She sat down and covered her face with her hands. If she could only focus her thoughts, if she could only listen to reason, and to her own instincts, not to sentiment; if Aharon only understood the gravity of the situation. She got up and stroked the young man's head.

"Gershon my child, I'll give you some food for the road. My God be with you."

She decided to show her husband the letter. When he came home he noticed she was not her usual self.

"Don't worry, Rivka," he told her, "I just got back from the town hall. Zenig Tuss promised me he would do his best to calm the situation."

An explosion was heard, and a large stone landed in the middle of the living room. Aharon rushed at the broken window, forgetting his disability. In the street he saw the two sons of the farmer Pihudka, their neighbor.

"Dirty Jews," they shouted. "Father says that your end is near. Death to the Jews, death to the Bolsheviks."

Aharon ran outside, waving his cane at them, threatening to beat them. The two ran back into the house. When Aharon came back Rivka was standing with Gershon at her side.

"Read," she said. His face turned white, but he kept calm. He wanted to talk to her in private, and they went up to the attic. Aharon said, "If this is true, then we are in great trouble. In my worst dreams I hadn't expected things to turn out this way." Suddenly he burst out crying and said, "What will happen to all the poor people who remained in town because of me? I am sick and my days are numbered; if they kill me, nothing will change. But you, Rivka, and Hannale and Eju, you must run away as soon as possible."

"No, father," came Hannale's voice as she climbed the ladder to the attic. "We won't leave you alone. We are a family and we will stay together for better or worse."

"Be quiet, Hannale," her mother ordered. "Join Gershon at dawn and run to the east, as far away as possible. I am an old woman. I will stay here in my birthplace with my husband."

"I won't leave you here alone, Mama, no matter what happens."

Night fell and a strange calm descended on the town. Even the farmers' dogs didn't bark, as if they knew what was about to happen. Hannale lay bundled in her bed. Her thoughts raced like a train going nowhere. Finally she fell asleep, exhausted. Suddenly a tank appeared in a storm. She was standing on Mickiewicz Street in Lvov, talking to Nushka. The tank came near, threatening with its cannon. She was paralyzed.

"I'm about to be run over," she yelled at Nushka,

"Hurry up, Hannale, run away."

"My feet are heavy," she said.

The tank remained and a cloud of dust made her cough. The turret opened and Vasily came out. He had no arms.

"Where is Haim?" she screamed.

"The war is lost," he told her. "Can I have some of your mother's dumplings?"

Suddenly her mother appeared, screaming for joy. "I knew you'd come back and save us."

"No," Vasily said, "I cannot save Aharon, he is an enemy of the Communists.

"Very well," she said, "I will bring you some dumplings and we can start out immediately."

"Traitor," Hannale shouted. "How can you abandon Father? Haim, my Haimke, come and save me. Everyone has a savior assigned to him by the Almighty."

"Haim will never come because of your father," Vasily answered. His roaring laughter grew louder. "Come, Rivka."

Enraged, she climbed the tank and started beating him. Suddenly she saw her mother running. She had two artificial hands and was saying, "Here, Vasily, Rivka will take care of all your needs." He started to push her away, and she fell and hurt her face. Hannale woke up in a panic; her heart pounded. She touched her face and was happy to find that it didn't hurt. She forgot the dream and fell into a dreamless sleep.

When the family awoke, there was no trace of Gershon. It was a clear day. The sun was shining brightly. As they gathered for breakfast, Aharon was quiet and withdrawn. Eju and Hannale were whispering to each other when they heard horses galloping. A luxurious carriage stopped in front of their house. Avremele the jeweler stepped down. His face was grave.

Rivka's heart began to race when she saw Avremele's pale, drawn face. It had been a long time since she had heard from her daughter and son-in-law. After their honeymoon, they had stayed in Kotzov, a charming town surrounded by the bright ridges of the Carpathian Mountains.

Avremele refused her offer of refreshment and began to speak, avoiding everyone's eyes.

"I have found out that the Germans reached Kotzov. The Jews there, including my son and your daughter, tried to escape. Anshel was able to reach Romania, but Ziporah was caught. On the same day the Germans assembled the few remaining Jews in the town and shot them to death in front of a large crowd."

Rivka fainted on the spot. When she was revived with cold water, she started to cry, "*Gevalt*, no, God in heaven, not Ziporah. Take me first, I beg of You." She went down on hear knees and cried bitterly.

Avremele patted her head and added, "I don't know if this will bring you any consolation, but I have it on good authority that your daughter was very brave. Moments before she was shot she spat in the face of the German officer, and when she was put against the wall she shouted, first in German and then in Hebrew, "The Eternity of Israel will not fail."

There was silence. Eju ran and embraced his mother. Hannale hugged and kissed her father. Avremele turned and left. To their amazement, the Hochbergs found that he had left a bundle filled with gold jewelry on their table. Mournful, each went off to be alone with his sorrow. Hannale grief was replaced with an anger that grew stronger and stronger. "It is not possible," she told her brother, "that people are executed for the sole crime of being Jewish."

"I think Papa understands now how serious the situation is, but there is nothing he can do," blurted Eju, who felt growing compassion for his father. As the youngest child and a good student who was fluent in

Hebrew, he would impress his father with Hebrew sayings and aphorisms. Thinking now about his oldest sister, he could not believe she was no longer alive. Only yesterday he had seen her thick braids. He remembered her wistful smile. How he loved her bedtime stories.

"You believe Ziporah is dead?" he asked Hannale. She did not answer. Until now the news had not sunk in. Now she began to realize what had happened.

"Yes," she said, "she died a heroic death. But no, it is not possible. She is my sister. She couldn't have left us. I am so confused, Eju, I don't know what to think."

"Papa and his German culture," Eju raged.

"Hush, don't upset him," she scolded.

"I should have run away with Munyu and joined the Red Army."

"You're only fifteen; how could they have drafted you?"

He ignored her remark, ran to his room and slammed the door. Hannale returned to the living room. Her father was seated, bent. His eyes were lowered. She turned to him.

"Papa, when the Germans arrive you will probably represent the Jewish community of Glinyany. Be strong; you will be given an important role."

He looked at her.

"I am happy to have a daughter like you. I will my best, Hannale. Go console your mother."


It was almost the month of Adar, but no one expected the feast of Purim to be observed that year. The wicked Haman was at the gate, and there was no hope for the arrival of Queen Esther or Mordecai the Jew. The mood was unbearable. Acts of hatred and destruction were increasing. The Ukrainians became wild, and it was clear the Germans were near.

It was Friday. The holiness of the Sabbath began to be felt. Ostensibly, preparations for the Sabbath went on as usual. The storekeepers began to close the stores and greeted one another with *Gut Shabbos*. Then a column of armored cars entered the town, painted with unusual black crosses. As if by magic, hundreds of people began to line the sides of the road leading to the town hall. Blue and yellow ribbons were seen everywhere. The Ukrainians, as well as a few Poles, stood by and watched the strange caravan.

Suddenly someone shouted, "These are the Germans. Long live the Nazi Empire our savior. Down with Bolsheviks and Jews." The crowd became excited. Flowers and sweets showered down from the rooftops onto the heads of the soldiers, who were wearing battle fatigues and waving to the crowd. Suddenly a huge blue and yellow flag was hoisted, along with the red and black swastika flag. "Long live Germany, *heil* Hitler!" the crowd shouted.

The Jews hid in their homes, trembling with fear. Through the drawn curtain Hannale observed a jeep stopping in front of the town hall. The tanks that followed it seemed light and fast compared to the clumsy tanks in Haim's unit. Two officers in battle fatigues, wearing high, visored caps, got out of the jeep. Zenig Tuss, who had appointed himself mayor of the town during the transition period, rushed towards them. They saluted him with raised hands, and he tried unsuccessfully to imitate them.

"The residents of Glinyany salute the famous German Army. We are happy to be liberated at last from the yoke of Bolshevism and Communism. The Ukrainian militia and national movement are at your service."

A young interpreter transmitted the message to the officers. They proceeded inside like lords and masters of the place, not bothering to return the greetings. The Germans moved their vehicles in perfect order. Young, expressionless soldiers huddled near the town hall, some of them smoking. The town children started to march with wooden sticks, blue and yellow bands on their arms. Suddenly they dispersed and started to yell, "*Zyd, Zyd.*" They headed for Motl, the youngest son of Itche, the butcher. Motl had been curious and he came outside to look at the column. When he saw the Ukrainian children running towards him, he started to run, but it was too late. They cursed him and struck him with their sticks. He fell unconscious on the ground as they fell back into a column and started to march. The next day Dr. Nass pronounced him dead. Motl's mother went into a deep depression, and the doctor had to be summoned again. Shaking his head, he said, "I have no remedy for the sorrow of losing a son." There were tears in his eyes as he wrote a prescription for some tranquilizers. After Motl's death, the Jewish mothers made sure their children did not leave home without an escort.

A few days after the arrival of the Germans there was relative calm. The Ukrainians stopped their harassment, as if waiting for orders from their new masters. Aharon's face softened and relaxed. He had been so troubled lately. He felt somewhat vindicated, as if he could now say, You see, I told you so. This is not a barbarian nation.

Hannale did not share her father's feelings. She knew this was the calm before the storm. The Germans' blank faces scared her. She had never before seen so much blond hair and blue eyes. Their eyes were cold and unfeeling. They looked like victors. Their uniforms were ironed and spotless. It was clear they despised the Ukrainians and were put off by them. Hannale, who knew German well, kept hearing them say, "These Ukrainian pigs are not much different from the Bolsheviks." But their instructions seemed clear: They were to respect the Ukrainian national movement and support it as an auxiliary force for the Wehrmacht and the SS.

A few days after the arrival of the German army in Glinyany, there was loud knocking on the door of the Hochberg family. Their neighbor, Pihurka, was standing there.

"I was ordered by the authorities to bring you over for questioning," he said. He was wearing brown gendarme uniform and cap, with a blue and yellow band on his arm. There were several armed militiamen with him.

"Ivan," Aharon spoke softly, "we are old neighbors, your children grew up with my children. I have always liked you. . . ."

Ivan Pihurka cut him short. "Don't make me take you by force. Come with me at once."

Aharon was barely able to say goodbye to his wife or children. He went out with them and marched towards the town hall. They were careful not to push him, as they still respected him and knew of his illness. When they arrived at the town hall he was shown immediately into the Mayor's office.

"Sit down," Zenig Tuss said in Ukrainian. In the corner of the room stood a German officer with close-cropped hair, who seemed about forty years of age. He wore the Wehrmacht's battle fatigues and his expression was severe.

Instinctively Aharon extended his hand to the officer and greeted him in flawless German. The officer seemed taken aback and almost extended his hand, but withdrew it immediately, his face frozen in forbidding lines.

"Sit down," repeated Zenig Tuss. He was angry he could not speak German and needed an interpreter.

"This is Major Berger of the Fifth Panzer Division," he said. "The German forces are on their way to rout the treacherous Russian army. According to the major, they have a serious obstacle on their way east because the Red Army blew up a big bridge on the way to Lvov. The division command has decided to build an alternate bridge. You must recruit 300 strong, young Jews for this task. The army wishes to start the work without delay."

Aharon was amazed. He replied in Ukrainian, "I have no authority to dictate to the young men of the town to go and work for the Wehrmacht." He turned to the officer and said in German, "Your honor must understand that most of our sons have families which, as fathers and sons, are their primary responsibility."

The major seemed angry. His face turned red but remained expressionless as he responded,

"Little Jew, listen to me, you have exactly two days to recruit the necessary manpower. Otherwise, we will unleash our Ukrainian friends and let them do whatever they wish with you. As far as I know, they have suffered enough at the hands of the Jews and the Bolsheviks and they are aching to avenge themselves."

The interpreter whispered something in Zenig Tuss's ear. The mayor turned to Aharon and slapped him across the face. Aharon fell down. With the help of his cane, he rose, incredulous. He had known Tuss for years, and would never have dreamed that such thing was possible. He limped away when he heard Major Berger's voice: "This is only a sample. Only two more days."

When Aharon got home he was speechless. He sat in his library, half unconscious, and remained silent for many hours. Rivka knew what he was going through and didn't say a word. Finally Hannale approached him and said,

"I know they hit you, Papa. Word has gotten around. We have also found out about the recruitment of men for work. Please, Papa, summon the rest of the Zionist Committee members and discuss the situation."

"I can't," Aharon said, covering his face. "Many of them are busy with their families and children; how can we decide who goes to work and who stays home?"

"Well, Papa, then I will have to go work. I am strong and I can work. If you don't call the committee I'll go to the town hall to volunteer."

Her determination alarmed him, and he collected himself.

"Go ahead, Hannale, bring them to the committee house."

When Aharon stood before the committee, he felt guilty. Their eyes made him suffer. He felt he was deceiving them. To his surprise, no one complained.

"Our dear Aharon, what shall we do?" they pleaded, as if he were their savior. Sensing their helplessness, he felt self-confident again. He said,

"My friends, I know what you are going through, but now you face a much more difficult task."

Most of the committee members knew what it was all about, but they listened to him respectfully.

"We have to come up with 300 workers in two days, to help the German army build a bridge outside town. The men have to be able bodied. My dear brothers, I don't know how we can do it, and I am asking for your help."

A commotion started. A man said,

"Most of our sons were taken by the Red Army, and the rest are busy with their families. We won't be able to endure these decrees, Aharon."

He knew they were right. He also considered the mission impossible. But he felt a responsibility towards these people. They continued to complain as Hannale whispered in her father's ear,

"Papa, I will make a list of all the able-bodied young men, and I'll read it to them."

"No, Hannale," he said. "They have to volunteer, we cannot enforce any kind of a list."

He asked for the floor, and everyone grew quiet.

"Tomorrow at sundown we'll gather again. There is no need for the entire community to gather. Only the council members will convene, and we will make our final decision."

After the men had dispersed, he remained seated with Hannale at his side. They were silent. They knew hard times were before them. They realized the gravity of the situation and felt terribly pessimistic. Finally they stood up, looked at each other without a word, and headed home. It was dark outside and the ailing man was cold. He put his arm around his daughter and said,

"Whatever happens, Hannale, be sure to reach Zion." She didn't answer. She felt sorry for him, realizing that his life was ruined. She admired him for his honesty and felt his pain. She could tell he was guilt-ridden. Hannale began to sing one of her father's favorite Hebrew songs, and saw his eyes grow misty. When they got home Rivka was still wearing her apron and cleaning the dinner pots.

"Why are you happy?" she asked when she saw their glowing faces.

"Our children will reach Zion," he said, "and will continue the tradition of their fathers."

"What does Zion have to do with the evil decrees awaiting us?" she wondered, but decided not to upset him. "Well," she said, "did you raise the labor force?"

"With God's help," Aharon said. He had never used this expression before, which made her worry.

"Mama, tomorrow the council will meet and appoint several candidates for work; Papa decided that the men will have to volunteer." Hannale spoke with forced optimism, which her listeners did not share.

The mood was somber, and all of Hannale's attempts to cheer up her family failed. Everyone went to bed. Rivka put out the oil lamps and went to her bedroom, but she couldn't fall asleep. She was gripped by a nagging restlessness. She decided to peek through the window. There was a full moon. The town was enveloped by a strange quiet. She felt trapped. She had never before felt death so close and threatening. She could see the blue and yellow flags waving over the Ukrainian rooftops. Even their dogs didn't bark, and not a soul was in the streets. She was afraid of what might happen next. Scenes of atrocities danced vaguely before her eyes. She was confused, gripped by a catatonic paralysis. She didn't even have the strength to feel bitter about her fate, or to imagine what would have happened if they had run for their lives before the arrival of the Germans.

Suddenly everything changed. Green vistas unfolded before her. Farmers were tilling their fields. She was sitting with her family around a table laden with delicacies. Aharon and Munyu were reading the *Book of Judges*. Hannale and Eju were playing outside. They were small. Ziporah was deep in conversation with Vasily, who was dressed in ceremonial uniform with many medals on his chest. She sighed with relief and fell asleep with a faint smile on her lips.

The next day, when the Jewish Council members gathered, tempers flared up again, and Aharon became the butt of criticism.

"We have a list of only fifty volunteers," Dr. Biliger began. "Tell the Germans we cannot recruit another person."

"Let's see how the members of this enlightened culture react," someone interjected.

Aharon did not respond. He asked them to await his return and started out toward the town hall. He did not see the major, but he submitted the list to a junior official and was told to wait at the council house. About 2 hours later, which seemed like an eternity, the sound of vehicles was heard approaching the house. The house was suddenly surrounded by armed soldiers, including members of the Ukrainian militia. Several gendarmes were carrying cans of fuel. Major Berger and Zenig Tuss marched towards the door. Soldiers were carrying bundles of straw, which they scattered around the house. Zenig Tuss said in Ukrainian,

"By army order you must supply 300 able-bodied volunteers within three hours."

Aharon turned directly to the major.

"Officer, sir, I beg of you, we were barely able to recruit fifty of our best young men. We won't be able to meet the high quota you've given us."

The major did not reply. He looked disturbed, turned on his heels and left, muttering orders in German. Zenig Tuss remained. He changed his tone of voice.

"As a friend I advise you to listen to the army's instructions. It cannot advance because of the blown-up bridge. Your lives are in danger."

"There is no way we can do it," Aharon interrupted angrily, "and no one knows it better than you."

"You will be sorry," Zenig said and walked out in a huff.

A few moments later the men inside the house became aware of the smell of fire. They looked out the windows and saw bundles of straw burning on the north side of the house. Flames began to shoot up. They started to cough; cries of "*Shema Yisrael*" rang out.

"Stop it!" Aharon thundered. "If we must die, let us die like our martyrs in Spain. Let us pray the confessional prayer."

The news spread around town. Gentiles and Jews rushed to the house and looked at the flames. The young knew that the fate of the men inside was sealed if something was not done quickly. Pesyeh, the butcher's son, young and corpulent, stepped forward and roared,

"Brothers, we must save these people." All the work volunteers stepped to the front of the house. Slowly, the young Jews began to move towards Pesyeh. The right number seemed to have been achieved.

"Zenig, put out the fire. We are ready to go to work."

The militiamen began putting out the fire and soon controlled over it. When they went inside they saw Aharon and the council members praying. Their spirits were strong.

"Papa, everything's fine," Hannale shouted. "The men are going to work."

He continued to pray as if he didn't see her. Slowly, everyone calmed down. Families evacuated their loved ones and everyone felt proud.

Life was becoming unbearable. With the young men away working on building the bridge, the burden of making a living fell on the women and children, who could not cope with the work load. Food became scarce. It seemed that the farmers preferred to join the militia rather than till their fields and their crops decreased considerably. The town's poor started begging and their children starved.

The Hochberg household was rather comfortable. Although food was not bountiful, there was enough for the family. Rivka would sigh from time and time, thanking God for having let Vasily stay at their house, since their sugar and flour were part of the Red Army's supplies. Major Berger was replaced by Captain Schlemberg, a reserve officer at war for the second time. He was a quiet, moderate man charged with organizing the local government in cooperation with the various nationalities in the region. In this capacity he conducted long talks with Aharon in German. The two took to each other and would often joke. When there was no one around, the captain whispered in Aharon's ear,

"I cannot believe such a thing can take place. I have seen what they did to your people in other parts of Poland. Good heavens, this is intolerable."

But whenever a Ukrainian entered the room he would change his tone of voice. He was particularly afraid of the SS men. Aharon had first seen them at the town hall, where he had been summoned urgently. They were tall, with black uniforms and shining boots, and their visored hats had the sign of a skull. On their sleeve they wore a red ribbon with a strange sign resembling a cross. Their eyes were cold and their presence threatening. The oldest one, a captain, was talking in a low voice to Schlemberg. He was introduced to Aharon as the person in charge of the SS in the region. His name was Kampke, and judging from his accent Aharon concluded that his was a Schwab, a German who had lived in Poland before the war. He held a whip. Aharon wondered why he had come in a military vehicle rather than on horseback.

"The SS is setting up a labor camp some 20 miles north of town," Schlemberg explained. "All the young men who worked on building the bridge will be transferred to that camp." Aharon instinctively refrained from protesting and continued to listen politely. "To help the war effort, the residents of the town must come up within a week with a sum equal to 50,000 *zlote*, in silver, gold, or any other valuables."

"I will do the best I can, Herr Capitan," Aharon said in perfect German, which surprised the SS man.

"Do you have an Aryan blood?" Kampke asked with a derisive smile.

"Who knows, perhaps," Aharon said, and mentioned his service in the Austrian army during World War One.

"My brother also fought the Russians at that time," the SS said and, surprisingly, asked for details about Aharon's service. The conversation was short and the message was clear. The community had to raise a huge sum of money in a short time.

The council convened immediately, and when the new decrees were announced there was general dismay and loud protests. The greatest anger was caused by the announcement that the young men would not be allowed to come back to town. Things were difficult as it was, and many families starved. There was no solidarity or equitable distribution of resources. The affluent did not help the needy, despite their constant pleading. Under such conditions, it did not look like the money could be raised. Finally Aharon said,

"I will go and talk to the families. It's the only way."

Despite all the difficulties, he was able to persuade the affluent people to contribute their share. To everyone's surprise, Aharon arrived in time at the town hall with the decreed amount. The events of the past month were vivid in his mind, and he knew that they would fulfill their threats, as they had when they nearly burned down the council house with all the people inside.

There was a relative calm in the town. The Ukrainians all but stopped their harassment. But the future remained uncertain. The food supplies continued to dwindle, and there were even some deaths. Rivka, afraid of what might follow, began to ration the food served to her family. Hannale didn't leave the house very often; she spent most of her time in her father's library, voraciously reading everything she could find. She was so busy escaping from reality that she didn't realize she had stopped menstruating until several months later. She consulted her mother and was told not to worry; it was not unusual, and might be the result of her anxieties about the future.

Stories of atrocities at the labor camp in Kurowice near Przemyslany began to reach town. Mothers and wives learned of the deaths of their sons and husbands. Aharon found out that the camp was run by the SS, headed by none other than Captain Kampke. There were stories of executions by shooting or hanging for the slightest offense. Other died because of hunger and hard labor. Most of the news was brought to town by Ukrainians involved in the war effort or employed as camp guards. But the people of Glinyany, led by Aharon, continued to hope for better times. The fact that the town was run by Schlemberg and reserve gendarmes made life somewhat easier and infused a feeling of relative safety, shaken at times by the visits of the commandant of the nearby labor camp.

It was a gray day. There was a constant drizzle, and an occasional ray of sun peeked through the clouds. It was neither cold nor hot. Few people were in the streets.

"What an indecisive day," Hannale reflected as she watched the weather. She went out to fetch water from the well. As she returned, she saw a group of Ukrainian militiamen, some of whom she recognized, marching towards her house. She rushed inside and called her father. The militiamen did not bother to knock on the door, enterering abruptly and ordering Aharon to come with them. He put on his hat and went outside. When he came back his voice trembled with emotion. He had a red mark on his face. Rivka was alarmed. She quickly dressed his face. He was sullen, disregarding the pain.

"This is it," he said. "We must leave Glinyany within four days. We have several alternatives. The Germans have established ghettos in the nearby cities, where they are herding all the Jews."

"Four days," Rivka whispered in fear. "We shall leave our house and all our belongings, and go where?"

"Well," Aharon said, "we shall go to the Przemyslany ghetto. We have many relatives in that town. We should be able to find a place."

"But they know nothing about this. How will tell them in time?" Rivka asked.

"We may not be able to reach them," Aharon said. "We may have no choice except to show up and hope everything will be all right."

They rushed to pack their belongings. "I'll talk to Leibl the wagon driver and try to get a wagon. We should be able to find shelter with Rolah."

The family quickly joined in the preparations. There was no time to be sad or to become too emotional. Everything was done quickly and efficiently.

As they sat in the wagon drawn by two strong horses that seemed to have been spared from hunger, Hanale had a feeling of *deja vu*. Suddenly she remembered Haim. It seemed she was traveling in the tank with him, and she felt at ease. But when she saw the rows of Ukrainians standing along the way with blue and yellow bands on their arms, she remembered the grim reality. She particularly angry at the militia members whom she recognized. She felt deceived and betrayed by the very people she had grown up with. She had lived in peace with them, and had never expected them to behave they way they did. At times it seemed that some of them lowered their eyes as the wagon passed by. The caravan of wagons was long, but after a while they were alone. The rest of the wagons headed for other destinations, to other ghettos in the surrounding towns. The family did not even bother to look back at their town and home, receding into the distance. It was scary how, within a few seconds, their past was erased, as if their lives had no significance. Their entire large family and their many friends had been ground into dust before their eyes, disappearing in the wind. But they did not shed a tear. They were too afraid of what what to follow. Each had a feeling of doom, but no one dare speak about it. They accepted their fate and made peace with it, though wishing to control and change it. A deep silence enveloped them as night fell. Aharon and Eju fell asleep, while Hannale and her mother were awake. They did not exchange a word; they knew what the other felt. Before daybreak they fell asleep, leaning on the few belongings they had taken with them. It was a sleep without dreams.

When Hannale woke up the sun was shining in the broad daylight. She had never been to Pshmishlana, and wondered what the town looked like. They did know these relataives, who had visited them frequently at their home, so did not feel as an unwelcome guest. The wagon reached the outskirts of town and was ordered to stop. A Ukrainian guard checked their papers and told them to join a caravan of wagons that was about to enter the ghetto. They were forbidden to dismount the wagon, even to relieve themselves. They waited many hours before they were allowed to enter the ghetto. The local houses did not impress Hannale. "This is not Lvov," she thought. Her parents knew the town well and even tried to identify the streets and squares. They were seized by a strange mirth Hannale was unable to share. Finally they reached the ghetto. Aharon turned pale and said to his wife,

"Good heavens, Rivka, look, the entire area is fenced in and closed and has changed beyond recognition. I cannot identify a single place."

The wagon reached the gate. Again there was an inspection, this time a stricter one, of their belongings. They were asked if they had brought any food with them. When they said yes they had to get off the wagon. They soldiers climbed on and overturned everything, confiscating whatever little food they could find. The family was asked for the address it was heading for; after this was given they were allowed into the ghetto.

The first scene Hannale came across was shocking. Although life in Glinyany seemed unbearable, with illnesses and deaths from under-nourishment, here in the ghetto the situation was beyond belief. Half naked children with swollen bellies and running noses sat by the road, begging for food. Rotting bodies were strewn along the road; no one bothered to remove them. People wore a yellow patch on their clothes with a Star of David inside—the word *Zyd.* The streets were packed with people, and the wagon driver could barely get through. The children's pleas and the rest of the scene shocked everyone. Hannale started to cry, and Eju started throwing them clothes, apologizing for not having any food. Aharon and Rivka looked at each other in amazement, beginning to grasp the enormity of the catasrophe.

Finally they reached their relatives' home. Roleh, Hannale's cousin, came running out to greet them. She was Hannale's age and was always full of joy. They embraced, and she helped them unpack their things. Her family lived on a side street, where they could not see the awful things they had seen before. For a moment it seemed like a normal visit. The rest of the family came out to greet them. They had not known about the visit of the Hochberg family, but rumors about the evacuation of the Jews from the villages to the cities had spread everywhere, and they assumed they would be having guests. Their mother gave everyone sheets and bedding and a bed to sleep in. It was a large, spacious house. In addition to the family, two acquaintances lived there, a physician and a pharmacist, both affable and pleasant. Aharon befriended the doctor and spent hours playing cards with him.

Hannale's mood improved greatly, although she did not leave the house for days on end. She enjoyed her cousin's company. Hannale told her cousin all about life at the school in Lvov and Haim. They laughed and sang together.

The general mood improved as well. Fortunately, there was no lack of flour and sugar at their relatives' home, and it was shared by all. The *Judenrat* (Jewish Council) of the ghetto, headed by Dr. Rotfeld, also rationed some of the food. While they did not always eat their fill, they did not starve. In addition, Roleh's brother and the pharmacist had jobs outside the ghetto, and from time to time could smuggle food past the strict controls. Sometimes the doctor received presents from Poles who had brought a sick child to the ghetto to be examined by him.

When the *Judenrat* heard of Aharon's arrival, it asked him to join the council. But Aharon refused in no uncertain terms, saying, "I failed completely in Glinyany when I advised my brothers to stay and not run for their lives. I am sick and my days are numbered. I am sure you are doing your job most efficiently, and I am also sure Hitler will lose the war. The Jewish people will survive, and everything will work out." Dr. Rotfeld had personally come to try to convince him. There were Jewish police in the ghetto who worked for the council and were under the orders of the Germans and Ukrainians. The Germans were not around; the Ukrainians guarded the ghetto and prevented any food smuggling. There was a sad kind of Jewish autonomy, which was well observed.

Hannale heard the work *Aktion* for the first time when her relatives rushed everyone to a hiding place under the cellar, which was perfectly camouflaged.

From time to time the Ukrainians or Poles leaked rumors about trucks arriving in the ghetto to take Jews according to a predetermined quota to be take to a place of liquidation. Several Jews who had survived mass shootings came to the ghetto. They told of having been taken to the train station in Przemyslany by trucks, loaded onto cattle cars and taken to Belzecz. There they were stripped naked, taken to trenches, and shot.

Some survived and crawled out of the trenches, where they saw bodies being buried in common graves or taken away to be burned. There were rumors about mass killings at Belzecz. The family started spending days on end in their hideout. At times they would hear steps and the voices of Ukrainians searching for them in order to evacuate them from the ghetto as part of the *Aktion.*

The number of people in the ghetto was reduced considerably, as was the crowdedness. But sanitary conditions were horrendous. Soon diseases began to spread among the residents. Aharon and Eju contracted typhus. Their temperatures rose and there were red blotches on their bellies. Little Eju was unconscious, while Aharon hallucinated. Rivka did not leave their sides. On the doctor's orders, their temperatures were reduced using wet sheets. There was no medicine available, and they were afraid to hospitalize them lest they be executed. "Besides, they don't have any medicine," the doctor said, and advised them to keep the patients at home. Then, suddenly, they recovered.

Things got worse every day. Throughout each *Aktion* Hannale remained in the hiding place. She would embrace her cousin and not utter a word. She felt the presence of the angel of death, and at times would feel his breath on her neck. She began to lose hope, believing the end was near.

After the third and largest *Aktion* the number of ghetto dwellers was sharply reduced. People started to move into the empty houses, and few people were seen in the streets. The family spent more and more time in the hiding place. One day Feige, a woman they had known well in Glinyany, about 23 years old, came to the house. Her husband had been taken to work during the first days of the occupation, and later sent to the Korowicze camp. Since then she had had no news of him. She had arrived at the ghetto in Przemyslany around the same time the Hochbergs had. During the third *Aktion* she was taken to the train station and then by cattle car to the Belzecz concentration camp. Many of the passengers had heard about the camp and the fate of its inamtes. After the train left the station she jumped off and saved her life, but she was afraid of the Poles and returned to the ghetto. Now she sought shelter and was let in without hesitation. They knew she had a year-old daughter, but did not ask about the child. Shortly after they learned that the young mother, in a state of confusion, had asked a woman on the train to hold her daughter and then saved her own life by jumping out of the window. They felt sorry for her, sharing her sorrow. No one criticized her. "We are not allowed to say anything. We were not in her shoes and we don't know what we would have done," Hannale whispered in her mother's ear.

But the story had a deep effect on the family, and they feeling of impending doom grew stronger. Finally they learned that very few families remained in the ghetto. Most of the people had been taken away during the raids, or had died from hunger and disease.

Roleh's brother stopped going to work. But he learned of a camp not far from the infamous Korowicze camp. There young Jews were engaged in sorting out the belongings of the liquidated ghetto. In the evening Aharon gathered the members of his family and said, with tears rolling down his face,

"My dear Rivka and my beloved children, I am old and sick and I will not be able to undertake a long journey. But I am sure you will be able to save yourselves. I have made up my mind. I am going back to Glinyany. Who knows, perhaps there is one righteous man in Sodom who will hide me. After all, all my life I was a friend of those Gentiles. Rivka, you are young and strong, go away with the children, and we will all meet in our home after the war."

"No, Aharon," she cried, "I won't leave you. My fate is your fate. The children will go work at the camp, but I am going back to Glinyany with you, come what may." She clung to him.

"Oh, well," he said, "we'll walk home then. Children, take care of yourselves. Go to Neibmlager and, as I said, I am sure we'll all survive."

They left before dawn. There was a quick farewell, and they did not take anything with them. To their surprise, no one stopped them. After walking for many hours they arrived in Glinyany.

"Hide here in the field," Aharon said to his wife. "I'll go into the village. No one will harm me."

He started walking down the main street, leaning on his cane yet walking upright. The Ukrainians stared at him from their windows, refusing to believe what they saw. "This Hochberg is a brave man," they said to each other. He decided to go to the town hall. There wasn't a German in sight. The news of Hochberg's arrival spread quickly. Some militiamen came over and stopped him. They tied his hands with a rope and ordered him to march towards the cemetery.

"Please let go of me," he pleaded. "Let me talk to Zenig Tuss."

"Shut up, dirty Jew," was the reply, "Zenig Tuss ordered us to arrest you. You are the enemy of the Reich and of the Ukrainian national movement."

When he reached the cemetery he saw his friend, Dr. Biliger. The latter's hands were also tied, and he was down on his knees. There were several stark naked men standing with their faces against the wall. He knew most of them.

"How did you get here?" Dr. Biliger asked him in a whisper.

"I wanted to find out if there was one righteous man in Sodom. It turns out that there isn't."

At that moment he was struck by a rifle butt blow which landed on his back and fell on the ground, losing consciousness for a few seconds. When he came to he heard the voices of the Ukrainians.

"Come and see, this dirty Jew has money." He was ordered to undress, and when they searched his clothes they saw the excrement pouch on the side of his stomach. They tore it off. When they saw its contents they started to beat him. They pushed their rifles into his exposed intenstines, which started to bleed. As they failed to find any treasure, they ordered him to start digging his own grave with his hands. In the distance Zenig Tuss was standing. He signaled to the soldiers by passing his hand across his neck, and Aharon was shot in the head, falling into the hole he had dug for himself. Next to be shot was Dr. Biliger. Both graves were covered over by the militia.

One of Pihurkah's daughters, hearing that Rivka was in the field, rushed over to her, crying, "My dear Rivka, I am ashamed of my people for having committed such a horrible crime. Your husband was executed by order of Zenig Tuss. Run for your life while there is still a chance. I know a hiding place. The miller is hiding a Jewish woman. I will ask him if he is willing to shelter you."

When Rivka heard the bitter news she sat down on the cold ground. She felt her life was no longer worth living. She asked the woman for paper and pen and wrote, "My dear children, I just found out that your father was executed. I am an old woman and I have no strength to go on living. When you get my letter I will no longer be alive. I am prepared to turn myself in. I would like to join your father. We were always together, and now we will be together forever. We will be free of this horrible suffering. Save yourselves. I am sure you will. Do not forget two things. First, tell the whole world about these atrocities and, second, avenge our blood and the blood of Ziporah and all the hapless souls who were murdered and their loved ones slaughtered. Remember, revenge, revenge, revenge."

She gave the letter to the Ukrainian woman and made her swear she would give it to a messenger who would deliver it to her children at the Neibmlager labor camp near Przemyslany. Then she stood up and started walking towards the cemetery, where she joined a group of Jews who had been captured after escaping from the ghettos in the region. A few hours later she was no longer among the living.

In the dark of night a group of young persons quietly left the Przemyslany ghetto. They walked briskly towards the Neibmlager on the outskirts of the town. Hannale was holding Eju's hand. She did not look back at the ghetto houses that receded behind them. There was a full moon, and their silhouettes were clearly visible. There was quiet in the town; not even the Ukrainian militia were seen in the streets.

"They must assume the city is clear of Jews," Hannale reflected. Suddenly she started worrying about her parents' fate. She did not tell her brother of her worries and continued to walk fast. At dawn they reached the camp and told the Ukrainian guard they were sent as reinforcement from the ghetto.

After the second *Aktion* the number of ghetto dwellers declined and a lot of property remained in the houses. Thus a labor camp called Neibmlager was established near the notorious Korowicze camp. Several young people from the ghetto were brought there; they worked exclusively at gathering and sorting the property. The camp commandant was a young officer named Appel, replacing the terrible Kampke, and the number of executions declined considerably. The mood in the camp improved, but people continued to die of starvation and disease. The guards at Neibmlager were members of the Ukrainian militia, overseen by German officers who did not belong to the SS.

When they arrived at the camp, Hannale's group was sent to the selection office. To her amazement, Schlemberg was sitting at a table next to his Ukrainian assistant. He looked at her in surprise and asked if she was the daughter of Aharon Hochberg of Glinyany. She eagerly confirmed this and asked him in German if he knew the fate of her parents, who had returned to Glinyany. When he said he didn't know she remained silent. "To the kitchen," he told his Ukrainian assistant, who sent her to the right.

When Eju and the others stepped forward, she said, "This is my brother and these are my sisters."

"Also to the kitchen," Schlemberg said and continued to sort out the new arrivals.

The work in the kitchen was considered the best, and although food was scarce and the individual rations meager, the kitchen workers were able to secure additional food for themselves from time to time. They also had the advantage of having a warm oven, which protected them from the severe cold outside.

The rest of the young people in the camp were busy sorting out all the property remaining in the ghetto, which was carefully accounted for. Valuables were confiscated at the order of the Germans, and taken by vehicles to an unknown destination.

The evacuation of the ghetto lasted for several months. The inmates knew that their survival depended on the continued need for this work. At times they would hear shots and cries, always from the direction of the nearby Kurowicze camp.

One day a young man arrived at the Neibmlager camp. Yaakov Kanner was the son of a large farming family which lived in various villages in the region. He was tall and strong, with blond hair and Aryan features. He had just escaped from the Kurowicze camp after strangling the Ukrainian guard watching him with his own hands. His brothers Itche,

Meir and Moshe were also strong and Aryan-looking, and were busy working on the evacuation of the Przemyslany ghetto. Yaakov had a superficial wound above his right temple. He said he had been shot while escaping, but the bullet had only scratched his head. He had not eaten for several days, and he quickly swallowed the little bread and soup which Hannale served him. He said, "The Germans are planning to liquidate the Kurowicze camp. The SS have started the executions. We have to organized ourselves and escape."

"Where to?" Eju asked.

"To the woods at Jachtorow," said Yaakov. "My brothers know the villages and woods in the area, and I know many hiding places." He was shivering with cold as he approached the burning oven. His curls shone in the fire. He looked haggard and spent, but determined to save his life. He had made contact with his brothers and sought to save them as well. Hannale took a liking to him. She dressed his wound and found a hiding place for him near the kitchen, where he awaited his brothers' arrival.

When they arrived everyone gathered again. Itze was the first one to speak.

"We must escape tomorrow night. We will leave through the north gate. About one hour after curfew, Hannale, Eju, Roleh, Gusta, Gitche, Monbach, Sonja, and Leibele will come quietly to our hut. Meir and I have knives and iron rods. Misha and Sergei usually stand guard there at night. The other night, when I passed by I heard loud snoring at their post, and I saw several empty vodka bottles. Hannale, see to it that they get their vodka and let's hope they are fast asleep. If necessary, we will have to dispose of them. We must take their rifles no matter what."

The next morning the men went out to work. Hannale waved goodbye at the Ukrainian guards who were on their way to the barracks after doing guard duty during the night. She smuggled three bottles of vodka to their barracks. They looked happy and grateful. "This may save their lives tonight," she thought. At noon a farm wagon with two horses passed the gatekeepers' residence. A woman in her sixties got off the wagon holding a letter, and asked for the whereabouts of Hannale Hochberg. She was directed to the kitchen. When she reached it she saw Hannale peeling potatoes. When Hannale lifted her head she recognized Ludemilla Pihurka, their old neighbor. She rejoiced at the sight of the letter. "Thank God they were saved," she said, about to embrace the woman, but then she noticed her stern expression and the glint of pity in her eyes. Hannale snatched the letter and started to read quickly. When she had finished, she felt a terrible void. The old Ukrainian peasant started to cry, but Hannale's throat was dry and the tears wouldn't come. She felt she was in a vacuum. The end seemed nearer than ever. She couldn't say a word. Her brother, who stood nearby, took the letter and read it. Then he seemed to go mad. He snatched a large kitchen knife and ran to the door, shouting, "Bastards, murderers, I'll make you pay, I'll kill you with my own hands."

With the help of some kitchen workers Hannale was able to stop him. He refused to calm down, swearing he would kill any Ukrainian he came across after he escaped from the camp. Finally Hannale thanked Ludmilla with all heart for the letter and the woman left. Hannale hid the letter in her clothes.

The new of their parents' deaths increased the group's determination to escape from the camp. But they felt this was their last chance. After dark they gathered at the hut of the Kanner brothers. They were afraid, but they knew they had nothing to lose. As the signal was given, the Kanners quietly approached the northern post. The two Ukrainian guards had drunk their fill of vodka but were still awake. They were struck on the back of the head with the iron rods and their rifles snatched from them. The north gate was opened and some twenty young people went out. They quickly headed for the woods. Yaakov Kanner walked with Hannale and Eju. He was still recovering from his ordeal at the Kurowicze camp. He leaned on Hannale and pushed her forward; when she slowed down he prompted her to keep in step. The group was led by Itche Kanner, who was thoroughly familiar with the surrounding area.

They walked all night towards the Jachtorow woods, and in the morning they reached a small clearing, where they divided into small groups. Each group had to dig a bunker in which to hide and sleep. They supported the roof of the bunker with logs and made themselves beds of rags filled with grass. The entrance to the bunker was a narrow opening with a ladder covered with dry twigs for camouflage.

Their daily life in the woods was governed by strict rules. They could not make fire or be seen in the clearing during the day. The Kanners made sure everyone followed the rules. They knew the area was full of Ukrainians and Poles who would not think twice of telling the Germans about them. A fire for cooking was lit inside the bunkers during the night so that the smoke wouldn't be seen outside.

The group obtained food from the farmers in the area. The men would raid their homes and, at gunpoint, take all the food they could get their hands on. They also took weapons from the farmers, and before long each one had his own rifle or pistol. At times they had to shoot a farmer who was resisting them, or who was known to turn in Jews. Occasionally they discovered that a Jew who had paid a farmer a large sum of money to be hidden on his farm had been turned over to the SS. They raided his house and executed him in front of his family. Eju took part in all these raids, both for finding food and revenge. He seemed to have matured. No longer was he the little boy clinging to his sister.

"Remember what Amalek did unto you," he kept saying to his sister, who worried a lot about his attitude toward justice, sometimes raising her voice. He protested the unjust distribution of food in the forest, which angered the other people in the bunker.

Winter arrived without prior notice. Heavy snow fell on the forest. The group spent more and more time in the bunkers, wrapped in coats made of odd pieces of clothes. Hannale was lucky enough to have a pair of leather boots which her brother had found during a raid. She and the others were afraid to go out and leave footmarks in the snow, which might lead the enemy to their hiding places. Their food supply started to dwindle, and fights broke out among the various groups. Yaakov Kanner continued to look after Hannale's and Eju's needs, even sharing his food with them. But their hunger gew worse, and it was decided that several people would look for food. When they returned they reported spotting German army units who, to their surprise, were moving westward. They had not obtained much food. The Polish farmer they had raided had told them that he and his family were starving too. But there was a sense of joy in the air, since the war seemed about to end soon.

The bunker dwellers split into groups or pairs which stayed together most of the time. Some male–female pairs began living as common-law married couples. (This happened naturally, with one invariably promising his mate to marry her after the war.) One of the young women became pregnant. She didn't tell anyone about it, and her swelling remained unnoticed because of her slimness. One day she gave birth to a beautiful baby, who kept crying because her mother did not have enough milk. The crying worried them; they were afraid they might be noticed. Some of them even threatened the mother and demanded that she get rid of her baby.

The snow began to thaw, and the group started sweeping it away from their bunker entrances and paths. They began to raid the farmers' houses more often and replenished their food supply. They always left a scout on one of the high trees to warn them of approaching danger.

By the end of winter and the beginning of spring the sun started to appear more often. The sky turned blue and the weather improved considerably, but the snow did not melt completely, and their bootmarks were clearly visible.

It was a clear, sunny day. As usual, they stayed in the woods near the clearing. Some were in the bunkers. Suddenly they heard the scout's familiar whistle. They rushed back into their underground lairs as they heard Ukrainian voices in the distance and the barking of dogs accompanied by commands in German. Startled, they began to hold one another. A guard stood, weapon ready, at the entrance to each bunker. The voices came closer. Suddenly the baby started to cry. The mother pressed it against her body as the people around her signaled her to keep it quiet. She tried to nurse the baby, but it continued to scream. Unable to quiet her down, she pressed her face against her breast. A burst of automatic fire was heard, then the thud of a body falling. Hannale began to tremble as her brother clutched his sawed-off shotgun and whispered in her ear, "Let me die with the Philistines."

They could clearly hear the steps of the search party above them, and they heard the Ukrainians talking to the farmer who had guided them.

"You said there were about fifty Jews here who have robbed you." The farmer confirmed this and told them he was sure he had brought them to the right place. Fortunately, the bootmarks in the woods led nowhere. Not a sound was heard underground. Finally their pursuers gave up the search. For hours they remained in the hiding place without budging. After nightfall they carefully crawled outside. Not too far from the bunker they saw the body of Eleh, the scout. His body was riddled with bullets. He had been unable to reach the bunker and had remained in his post, where he was discovered and shot. Everyone was fond of Eleh. He was eighteen, and his entire family had perished in the ghetto. He never fought with anyone, and always shared his bread with his comrades. He always volunteered to serve as scout and was a fast tree climber.

They stood there and looked at the body. They did not know what to say, nor did they have any tears to shed. Suddenly they heard a man crying. It was the baby's father. The distraught mother came out holding a tiny body which seemed asleep. She went down on her knees, mumbling, "She didn't even have a name." She placed the baby in Eleh's arms and said, "Take care of her, wherever you may be."

The father continued to sob and refused to be comforted. That night the two were buried in a common grave, while Eju said *Kaddish.*

With the final liquidation of the Kurowicze camp a considerable number of survivors reached the Jachtorow woods. They joined the various groups, and some dug their own bunkers in the area. Conditions grew crowded as did the squabbling. Discipline declined. Some even dared to make fires in the middle of the day.

"Carelessness will cost us our lives," Yaakov kept telling Hannale. But her mind was on her brother, who kept looking for perfect justice. At times he got himself into heated discussions which fortunately did not end in disaster. She kept asking him to calm down and give up his extreme ideas, but he wouldn't budge. He was a fearless fighter and took part in the most daring operations. His nickname was "Stavinsky" and, although the girls took a liking to him, he would blush whenever they called his name.

Their daily routine continued. People grew less and less afraid. They would start fires during the day and didn't bother to cover their trails. The local farmers knew that a large group of Jews was living in the woods, particularly since many of them had night visitors who took much of their food. It was also hard not to notice the smoke that rose above the woods and the smell of roasting meat. Some went to the German headquarters in Przemyslany and reported the presence of many Jews in the Jachtorow woods.

That day, Hannale had stayed in the bunker with Yaakov, who didn't feel well. They heard shots, followed by orders in Ukrainian to advance. The cries of the wounded were heard, then shouts to run in every direction. Hannale froze. Yaakov jumped up, took his weapon, and went outside.

"Don't go!" Hannale yelled, pulling his coat. They crawled back to the bottom of the bunker and covered themselves with a layer of clothes. The Ukrainian voices came closer, followed by orders in German. They heard the branches crack; then the hatch of the bunker was opened. Yaakov aimed his weapon. A grenade was tossed inside. Yaakov yanked Hannale toward himself, clung to the ground and buried her head in his bosom. The explosion was so loud than Hannale felt her eardrum rupture. She couldn't even say *Shema Yisrael*. Clods of soil landed on them but the bunker didn't collapse because of the heavy beams holding it up. They were still in each other's arms when they noticed the blood running down Yaakov's face. He kept clutching her against himself, and she felt his heartbeat. She was glad they were both alive and tried to treat his wound, but he told her not to move. After waiting for what seemed like an eternity, they got up and carefully crawled through the gap that had opened in the roof of the bunker. They had no idea what had happened to their friends. Darkness fell, and the ones who had managed to escape started returning. Hannale was overjoyed to see her brother return. In the morning they counted ten dead and buried them immediately.

The group decided to move to a deeper part of the woods. This time they took every precaution, and they continued to enforce the rules for several months. But complacency set in once again. The snow had melted completely by now, which made things easier both for them and for their enemies.

During the third raid on their hiding place Hannale was out in the woods picking blackberries with Roleh. When they heard shots, the two of them started to run.

"Run over there!" Roleh pointed at a thicket. They took shelter behind the bushes.

The tactics of the pursuers had not changed. First came the Ukrainians, who fired in every direction, and behind them marched the Germans. This time they had no dogs. They tossed hand grenades into the bunkers.

The two lay motionless on the ground. A few steps away they could see the boots of the soldiers; death seemed near. Hannale closed her eyes and waited for death to come. The pursuers kept marching and didn't stop.

When it grew dark they came out and returned to the bunker. There were many dead this time and morale was low. After discussing their situation they decided to move on in the woods. They tried to keep changing hiding places as often as they could. They were aware of the constant danger awaiting them, and observed the rules of caution to the point where they stopped making fires altogether. They had little food, but the will to survive remained strong.

One day a man named Yankele Fanger arrived. His family had lived near the village of Biala, and he knew the area well. He had never lived in the ghetto. When the Germans arrived he had found a hiding place for his mother and started wandering in the woods. He was tall, with dark, curly hair and huge muscles. Hearts filled with fear at his sight. He was hot-tempered to boot. The farmers in the area were afraid of him, having had a taste of his strength before the war had even started. It was rumored that he killed farmers at the slightest provocation. He wore a pistol in his belt and carried a short-barreled hunting gun on his shoulder. he wore German boots; no one knew where he had gotten them. His eyes flashed and kept moving. He spoke mainly Polish and knew little Yiddish and his sentences were short and choppy.

"It is dangerous here," he told them. "The Germans are retreating from the Russian soldiers, and from time to time they raid the surrounding woods. Russians who escaped from the German prisoner camp have started to organize, as have Polish partisans. I have heard about a Polish group that was planning to attack the Jews in this area. It would be better if you came with me to the forest near Biala. My mother is being hidden by Winczewic the forester, who promised to supply food."

Many were repelled by Fanger's appearance and by the rumors that had spread about him. Some said he was pretty crazy and would also kill Jews who didn't obey him. They were also tired of wandering and decided to overlook his warning.

"I go with him," Yaakov whispered in Hannale's ear. She hesitated. She, too, was afraid of him, but she knew that if they stayed in the Jachtorow woods they would not survive.

"What a charming man," Roleh said. She seemed to have been deeply impressed by him and had taken a liking to him. She got up and stood at his side.

"Come, let's go," Hannale said to Eju. He looked at her in amazement.

"With Fanger?" he asked, alarmed.

"Yes," she said. "Otherwise we will soon die." Yaakov Kanner came along, as well as some young men and women.

It was a short farewell. No one shed a tear. They took their belongings and began to follow Fanger. He was a fast walker, and from time to time he told them in a gruff voice to hurry up. No one dared disobey him. They walked all night. Fanger knew all the roads and every corner of the forest. Sometimes he would stop and listen. "A fox," he would say and continue to march at a fast pace. Finally they reached their destination, the village next to Biala. It was beginning to stir with the sounds of domestic animals.

Hannale walked next to Yaakov Kanner, holding his hand. He gave her a feeling of security. She knew he had lost his wife and two daughters, who had been taken from the ghetto of Przemyslany to the Belzecz death camp. He did not speak about it, but one could see his pain in his face and in his sad expression. Sometimes he would smile at Hannale, and she knew what was going on in his heart. Yaakov was older than the others, level-headed and liked by all. He had been the only one of his brothers who had been sent to Lvov to study. He was going to study law, but the war had cut his studies short and he was forced to return to the village. He was well-spoken, and never took part in the frequent arguments in the woods. He would always compromise and try to make peace. Although his character was the opposite of Yankl Fanger's, in his heart he admired him for his daring and courage.

"I wish we had many like him," he told Hannale, adding, "If there were more people like him, they would not have taken us like sheep to the slaughter."

Their place of hiding was on the edge of the woods, not far from the home of the forester Winczewic. Again, they dug a bunker, and their old daily routine was repeated. This time they had more food. In addition to having the forester's help, the men went out to look for food, which they usually took from the farmers. Sometimes they would be gone for days on end and Hannale would get worried, but they always returned with much booty. Her brother gave her boots and new riding pants for her twentieth birthday.

Men would return to the Jachtorow woods and would report on what was going on there. One day Yaakov told them that his brother had been joined by a large number of Russians who had escaped from German captivity. They had organized theselves and the Jewish men into a fighting partisan group. Their main mission was to attack retreating German army units. The group had been attacked by Polish partisans, and some of them, who had fought bravely, died in battle.

"I don't know who hates us more," he said, "the Germans, the Ukrainians, or the Poles. But when the war ends we'll take care of all of them."

Yankl Fanger and Roleh began acting like lovers, never leaving each other's side. Roleh joined the men in their operations, and even carried a firearm at all times. Hannale recoiled from guns, but she knew she would have to use them when the time came. Fanger was in charge, and nothing was done without his permission.

The bunker dwellers used to dry wet twigs on the oven they had built in the bunker. One day the bunker was filled with smoke and Hannale fainted. Fanger told Eju,

"She has typhus. We must take her out right away or we'll get sick."

Eju's pleas were to no avail. Hannele was removed from the bunker to the woods, and covered with coats and a layer of snow to keep her warm. Back in the bunker, Roleh and Yankl began to argue. He latter threatened to throw her out of the bunker too if she kept bothering him about Hannale. She started to cry, by he wouldn't budge.

Hannale woke up and started to breathe the pure air. The snow covering her had protected her from the harsh cold. Fortunately, the snow outside had stopped falling. Night fell, but everything was visible against the snow. Suddenly she felt immense relief. She had grown sick of the stifling bunker, the daily fights, the crowded conditions. Here she felt free, not like a prisoner in a pit. She started to remember. She remembered her parents; her mother's letter came back to her. Hannale's eyes filled with tears, and she felt rage, a desire to take revenge. "Tomorrow I'll go out with the men," she thought. She fell asleep, exhausted. When she woke up she knew she had dreamed but could not remember anything. It was the first time she had dreamed since war had broken out. She fell asleep again. When her brother woke her in the morning, she got up and laughed, to his surprise. He checked her forehead. She had no fever. She felt excellent. Eju went back to Fanger and begged him to let her back in the bunker. Fanger went to make sure she didn't have typhus. When Hannale saw him she smile brightly and said, "It's been a long time since I slept so well." Roleh, who had followed him, brought her a hot drink and said to Yankl, "She could have frozen to death because of your stupidity."

He did not respond and turned away. Hannale followed him.

"I am not angry at you," she said. "On the contrary, I had a very good night. I would like to go out with the men tonight."

Fanger stopped and loked at her, astonished.

"What for?" he asked. "Stavinsky and Kanner take care of all your needs."

"This is not the point," she said. "I would like to avenge the death of my parents."

He nodded and took out his pistol.

"Here," he said. "You're a woman after my own heart. I used to think you are one of those cowardly Jews who were butchered by those sons of bitches without doing a thing about it." He spat on the ground. "They are a shame to our people. If Joshua bin Nun saw what's been going on here he would turn in his grave." His voice deepened with anger. She thought he had said, "Jesus Christ," but she realized what he meant— Moses' follower. Suddenly she looked upon him as an ancient Hebrew leader calling his people to revolt.

"You are my Bar Kochva," she told him. "I am at your service."

He had never heard of this ancient Jewish hero who had rebelled against the Romans. He listened patiently as she told him about Bar Kochva and his face brightened. He seemed to have heard that story long ago. When she was done he got up and showed her how to use the pistol.

That night they went out together, heading for the home of the Ukrainian hunchback who lived not far from Biala.

"He killed a Jewish woman and her son with his own hands after hiding them for a large sum of money," Wiczewic the forester had told Fanger. When they reached the house the dogs started to bark and the donkey brayed in the stable. Fanger threw meat to the dogs, which made them quiet down. They kicked the door open and saw the twisted figure of the hunchback. In addition to his deformity, he had the pockmarked face of a leper. His mouth drooled; there was an awful stench in the room. Hannale felt sick. Her aversion was mixed with pity for this handicapped person, who went on sleeping as if nothing were going on. Fanger poked him awake with his rifle butt.

"Where are the flour and the sugar?" he asked the hunchback. The man was frightened and started shaking. There was a cold sweat on his forehead. His drooling intensified. He stammered something about not having any food, and a kick from behind sent him to the floor. The group discovered a small door which led to a staircase. Two men went down and came back.

"There is plenty of food down there," they said. When they brought up the sacks they found a teddy bear lying on the floor. Fanger picked it up and asked where it came from.

"By the Holy Virgin," the hunchback said, kneeling down, "they died of typhus."

"Liar," said Fanger, slapping his face. "You killed them. Winczewic told us all about you, and you will pay with your life. But you will have to suffer first." He took his knife and cut off the man's ear. He started to wail and the blood rushed to his face. Suddenly they heard voices speaking Ukrainian. Fanger shouted to Hannale, "The hour of revernge has come. Finish him off," and he went out quickly.

The men loaded the donkey. Hannale remained alone with the creature who was pleading for his life. She cocked the gun and aimed at his head. Her hand trembled. She had never killed a living creature, not even a fly. She had a kind and merciful soul, and didn't believe anyone had the right to take another's life. She was disturbed by her feelings of pity for the hunchback despite the fact that he killed a mother and child in cold blood. Suddenly she remembered her father; in her mind she saw him being executed. Did he ask for mercy? Did he plead for his life? How can people do such a thing? Her feelings were split and she felt immobilized. Beads of perspiration covered her face and her mind was in a turmoil as she fired. The hunchback closed his eyes; when he opened them he found that he was still alive. But he was still frightened.

"I won't be an animal like you people," she said. She shot a few more times in the air.

When she rejoined the men, Fanger slapped her on her shoulder. "You are a woman of valor," he said. For a moment she was sorry she had not carried out his order, but on second thought she told herself she was not made for killing.

The men rushed back into the woods, where they felt safer. The story of Hannale's bravery spread among the woods dwellers. She was praised by all, and her reputation rose sky high with Fanger, who started including her regularly in his operations.

Hannale became aware of a certain distancing on the part of Yaakov Kanner. It upset her, and one day she asked him about it.

"I don't know," he told her. "It seems that you are one of the people I stay away from and even object to."

She told him what had taken place at the home of the hunchback. He looked at her incredulously, then he smiled and said, "I knew you were incapable of such a thing." He held her. Suddenly he had a terrible thought.

"Remember how Fanger mentioned Winczwic's name to the hunchback?"

She thought about it. "Yes, why do you ask?"

He did not respond, but looked at her with growing fear. She knew what he was thinking.

"We must tell Fanger. After all, Winczewic is hiding his mother. We must warn him."

He got up and started walking towards Fanger.

"Stop," she cried, "he'll kill me for not obeying his order to kill the hunchback."

He stopped, not knowing what to say. He knew Fanger would kill her. He was uncompromising.

"We must think quickly and save Winczewic and Fanger's mother," he said. "Stop crying and help me think."

She said, "I'll go to Winczewic and tell him the truth."

"No," said Yaakov, "I'll go."

The forester was alerted and moved in with his brother on the other side of the woods. Fanger took his own mother with him. From now on they no longer felt safe in their hiding place. Fanger made contact with a group of Russian partisans and joined them in ambushing retreating German vehicles. From her hiding place Hannale could see the endless columns of slowly moving vehicles, sometimes drawn by horses. The soldiers looked tired and their uniforms were torn. There were many wounded, and the constant harassment by the partisans added to their troubles. The tanks moved slowly, no longer as shiny and threatening as she remembered them back in Glinyany.

"Look how the glorious German army looks," Kanner whispered to her. As he watched the soldiers he murmured, "What do these poor creatures have to do with Hitler?"

They would provide cover while their comrades fired on and charged the vehicles. They had many successes and few losses. The German army had lost its punch.

It was the spring of 1944. The acclaimed First Panzer Division reached the area, having retreated in perfect order from the Russian front. The men of the division were known for their fighting ability and daring. They were not too badly beaten by the Russians, but they had strictly obeyed the order to retreat. When they were attacked by the partisans they quickly regrouped for a couterattack.

The snow was completely gone, and the wheat fields were turning green. The farmers used every piece of land for growing wheat. The sun shone but the air was still cool. Springs filled with water and the singing of birds billed the treetops. There was a false sense of calm. Everyone felt the war was coming to an end, a feeling reinforced by the approaching roar of guns.

A German unit with a few Ukrainians approached the hunchback's home on the edge of the woods. They went into the house and, pulling him out, they demanded to know if there were any partisans in the vicinity. He was frightened and he showed them the missing ear as he cursed the dirty Jews who had done it to him.

"Some Jewish partisans are hiding near the forester's house," he said.

On that bright spring morning most of the bunker dwellers decided to sit outside and breathe the fresh air. They were busy with their daily chores, such as cleaning their weapons, while Hannale was having a lively conversation with Yaakov Kanner. Suddenly shots rang out. They jumped up as if bitten by a snake.

"Come with me!" yelled Yaakov, and they started running together. Eju disappeared in the woods as Yaakov pulling Hannale toward the wheat field.

"We must cross the wheat field to the next forest. There we'll be safe," he panted.

Hannale felt she was losing her breath.

"I can't go on," she said, falling. He picked her up and continued to run. After they reached the wheat field she fell again, exhausted. Yaakov started running again. Suddenly there were shots and he stopped. Hannale could tell he'd been shot in the neck as he collapsed in a pool of blood. She rose, shielding her head with her hands. Suddenly she felt pebbles hitting her; blood was running from her arm and breasts. As she fell she knew she had been shot. She could barely breathe as blood started to pour from her mouth. She lay motionless, her left arm still on her head, waiting for her death. She felt strangely calm. The sight of her own blood running and staining the wheat field didn't frighten her. She was sorry she didn't have a weapon and couldn't take down some enemies with her. How she envied Samson! She didn't feel pain, but breathed with great difficulty.

Hannale's calm was shattered when she saw a group of German soldiers walking nearby, following a Ukrainian militiaman who surveyed the area. When they saw the bodies of Kanner and Hannale they said, "They're dead." Hannale prayed that the Ukrainian would not be the first to examine her. Her heart pounded when a young medic came over. His left eye had been smashed, replaced by an ugly scar. But his good eye was kind and friendly. His sad face was tired and unshaved. He wore several gold rings on his delicate hands, which were miraculously clean, in total contrast to his worn-out uniform and torn boots. When he leaned over Hannale he was amazed to see her open eyes and helpless yet fearless gaze looking straight at him. "*Ein Maedschen*," he murmured, "a young woman," and seemed to be at a loss.

"I was wounded, the Ukrainians are after me, please don't turn me over to them," Hannale said in perfect German.

Greatly surprised, he asked how she knew German so well.

"It's the language we spoke at home," she said. "We also learned German in high school."

Marveling at her answer, he began to pity her. He was not sure whether she was Jewish or Schwabian. No, she didn't look Schwabian. A gypsy? They did not speak German. Who was she?

He decided not to ask any more questions and started to examine her wounds. She was overcome by nausea and started vomiting blood. The soldiers nearby started looking in their gear and found some bandages. They gave them to the medic, who started cleaning and dressing her wounds. He took a bottle of ether from his pocket, poured some on a bandage and put it near her face. She felt somewhat relieved and stopped vomiting. Her mind blurred as she heard him ask, "Where are the rest?"

"There is no one here except for me and my friend who was killed," she replied. Carefully, they put her on a stretcher. Four soldiers carried her towards a wagon drawn by two horses, waiting on the side of the road. They took her to the village of Biala. On the way the medic leaned over her and said,

"My name is Laurence, what is yours?"

She moaned with pain as the wagon kept jerking. He put his coat under her head and took some dry bread from his bag.

"Here, have some Hitler cookies," he laughed. She shook her head and closed her eyes, then opened them again when she heard an officer cursing the war and Hitler.

"Everything will end soon," Laurence whispered to her. "I fear for the fate of my wife and children. Rumor has it Leipzig was bombed mercilessly. Their last letter arrived a month ago."

There was a tear in the corner of his eye. Hannale rubbed her own eyes in disbelief. "A German soldier with wife and children, how is it possible?" She was amazed by the intensity of the pity she felt for him. She held him arm lightly and said, "I'm sure everything will be all right. The mail may be late in reaching the front."

He felt affection towards the wounded young woman lying on the bottom of the wagon. Deep down he knew she was Jewish. As they passed towns and villages he saw SS men rounding up her people. He knew about the mass murders. He could never understand it. He had been occupied with the savage battles taking place at that time, with treating the thousands of wounded and the victims of the cruel Russian winter. Now he recalled an incident during the retreat. He had been in charge of the train car for wounded. When his train stopped he saw bolted cattle cars and heard terrible cries coming from them. When he asked about them, he was told they were from children being evacuated from the ghetto. He saw many SS men and Ukrainian militiamen around the train. He was repelled by the black uniforms and skull insignia on their hats. Some of his townsfolk had joined the SS. "Human scum," he thought to himself. They were cold and closed and had threatening stares. They traveled on the trail of the Wehrmacht but seldom took part in the fighting. All they were concerned with was the Jews. They dressed impeccably and their boots shone. The army officers were afraid of them and closely followed their instructions. He despised them for collaborating with the Ukrainians. He was repelled by them; with their body odor, their rotting teeth, and their pig eyes dancing in their sockets. They looked dumb and treacherous as they giggled at the hapless souls locked in the cars knocking desperately on the doors and crying, "*Abiseleh vasser.*" It sounded like bad German, but he knew they were begging for a little water. When they were taken off the cars the Ukrainians pushed them savagely. A young woman started to run, clutching a child to her bosom. "Water," she begged. "My child didn't have a drink in two days." He would never forget how she was shot in the back by an SS. He covered his face as the memory came back, but he would never be able to rid himself of this terrible scene. Hannale could tell he was suffering. She caressed him with her eyes. When her pain intensified she he gave her a shot of morphine and she fell asleep.

When she woke up she was lying on a stretcher among dozens of wounded, mostly Wehrmacht soldiers who had been on the retreat. When her eyes began to focus she saw Laurence standing there talking to a giant in a white tunic who wore eyeglasses and a stethoscope. She knew he was a doctor. He noticed that she was awake and came over. Before he said anything she begged, "Please give me cyanide. I am tired of living. I can't keep on running from the Ukrainians and the SS. My entire family has been killed."

Although he had been told that she spoke German, he was amazed.

"Cyanide?" he asked, "How do you know about cyanide, and how did you learn how to speak German so well?"

"I've studied chemistry," she said. "If you have any mercy, please kill me."

"My name is Dr. Karl Musie," he said. "I am a physician and an officer of the Wehrmacht. I won't do it." His pale face was close to her; his blue eyes were tired and his gown was stained with blood. "You were hit by four bullets, with one remaining in your left lung. The rest were in your left arm and were taken out. The chest wound will heal and you will be well soon. I will help you."

"Where am I?" she whispered.

"In the field hospital of the *Erste Panzer Divizione* (First Tank Division). Hush," he said, as an SS armed with a submachine gun appeared.

"I came to take the wounded partisan."

Laurence was standing nearby. He looked on with mounting anxiety.

"The partisan cannot be transferred," the doctor said sternly. "She is unconscious." She closed her eyes and held her breath. The SS man looked at her somewhat suspiciously but didn't say a word.

"I'll be back soon," he said and raised his hand in salute. The doctor instructed Laurence to change her bandages. An ointment was put on her wounds. She was taken by some soldiers to an empty barn nearby and laid carefully on the straw. They placed straw under her head and covered her with a military blanket. The door was closed and she was left alone. She felt a slight pain in her left arm but she felt safe. It grew dark in the barn. She could see some stars through a crack in the ceiling. She put straw over her blanket. She didn't feel the cold. She was at ease, removed from reality, and for a moment she forgot the past and seemed to be in a another world, a kind world in which people respected one another, the enlightened world described by her father, a world of peace and calm. She imagined herself in a beautiful garden with brooks and water fountains, where everything was blooming and the fragrance of flowers filling the air. She was dressed in the white Sabbath dress her mother had made for her, and the lace trailed behind her. She was holding a bouquet of flowers she had picked. She was alone, singing a familiar song and dancing, and she lay down on the grass and fell asleep with a flower on her forehead.

She awoke with a start at midnight, blood running down her legs. She thought her wounds had started bleeding, but started to laugh as she realized she was menstruating. She hadn't menstruated in three years. She fell asleep again with a smile on her lips.

Next morning she met Walter Rosenkranz. He had entered the stable, sat down next to her, and waited for her to wake up. When Hannale awoke she saw a middle-aged man, corpulent, with gray eyes and graying temples. He wore unkempt officer's uniform and his boots were soiled. He didn't introduce himself, but both of them felt they had known each other under different circumstances. Hannale looked at him for a few seconds, saying a word. He looked at her blood-stained pants. She felt somewhat embarrassed. Finally Walter asked, "Who are you?"

She said without hesitation, "Hannale Hochberg. My father's name was Aharon, a proud Jew from Glinyany. My parents were murdered by the Ukrainians, and my sister. . . ."

"You are mistaken," he interrupted her. "This is not your name."

"Oh God, this is my name," she mumbled, squirming.

"What is your Polish name? You do have a Polish name, don't you?"

"Ana, Ana Stavinska," she said quickly, recalling her brother's nickname in the forest.

"Isn't it true that you are not from around here, but live far away?" he asked.

She started to understand that a miracle was taking place. She said, "It's true. I am from Voholin."

It was the birthplace of one of her schoolmates in Lvov. The officer sighed with relief and continue to write down her words.

"According to your testimony, after you were wounded you were alone except for that unlucky man who was killed in the woods. Am I right?"

She nodded, unable to speak.

"My name is Walter Rosenkranz. I am an intelligence officer of the First Panzer Division. You can rest now. You are safe here. He'll be back tomorrow."

Hannale almost called him to come back. She wanted to continue the conversation and ask him where he was from and who his family was, but he left abruptly. Her thoughts were interrupted when Laurence, the medic, walked in. He carried a package of Lignin. He gently helped her change her blood-soaked bandages and instructed her to use the Lignin for her womanly needs. How did he know? Did Walter send him?

Her curiosity about Walter would not let her fall asleep. Should she question him or not? She decided she would. When Walter walked in with his briefcase the next day, she smiled at him in gratitude. He remained serious.

"I know you are a kind person," she said, "but why would you help me and risk your life?"

Walter did not reply and kept looking at her with a sad expression. Finally he muttered, annoyed, "I'm just a person."

"Are you Jewish?"

"Must I be Jewish to be a human being? Aren't there any Germans who remained human during this ugly period? Just as Hitler is a disaster for the human race, he is even a greater disaster for Germany."

He stopped, smiling at her, and said, "Here." He handed her something wrapped in paper. When she opened it she was surprised to see a dress.

"I had one of the local women sew it last night."

"Thank you," she said. She felt like kissing him, but she was too weak.

"There is something else in the package," he said. She searched and found a yellow bathing suit.

"Wear the dress in the meantime," he said. "It is still cold on the Russian front and you can use this."

Hannale laughed when she discovered a package of dried fruit covered with chocolate. On the package it said in German, "Only for the front." She started to cry tears of joy and there was gratitude in her eyes as she said, "I haven't tasted anything like this in four years. She was afraid to eat, but Walter insisted.

"Eat, my child. Everything is about to collapse. Soon there will be no front. Germany is defeated. The Russians will be here in a few days."

She had mixed feelings. She felt safe with Walter around. She was happy whenever he came to see her, but she kept thinking that if she were in the woods with the rest of her friends, she might be liberated now from this entire nightmare. She started to worry. What would happen to her? Would she be able to remain with Walter until the liberation? Would he take her with him? She was afraid of the Ukrainians who were still roaming the area, armed.

He did not come back the next day. She remained in bed most of the time. She tried to crawl, but her pain increased. She was seized with fear whenever the door screeched. Two days later Walter returned, accompanied by Dr. Musie, who examined her and said, "Your wounds are healing fast. You are young and strong. Soon you'll be completely recovered." After he changed her bandages he whispered to Walter and then went out and left the two of them alone.

"The situation is getting worse," said Walter. There are armed gangs in the area. The army has completely lost control. We must transfer to a safer place."

"Walter," she said, "a Jewish woman is hiding at the home of the

forester Winczwic' her name is Fangerova. Please give her this letter."
  The letter said,

  Dear Mrs. Fanger,
  I am writing to you after being wounded and captured by the
  Germans. I am doing well, and I am sending you this letter with
  Walter Rosenkranz, an officer in the Wehrmacht. He is a great
  and enlightened man, truly an angel. He has helped me and saved
  me from the SS. Please send me some clothes and tell Yankl
  about me. Tell him the time of the liberation is near. The
  Russians are only a few days away. Give my love to Eju. The
  nightmare will end soon.

  Walter took the letter. He was very uneasy about doing it. He knew
what would happen to him if the SS found out about it. They were willing
to overlook many things. Sometimes they even smiled when derogatory
remarks were made about the Third Reich. But helping a Jew was
something that would never be forgiven. He could not recall anyone in
the Wehmacht ever doing something like this. He knew what happened
to local people who dared to hide Jews, and sometimes he watched with
disgust as they were shot.
  As he rode his bicycle to Winczwic's home, he thought about this
Jewish girl and wondered why he was risking his life for her. Was
there something about her that bewitched him? He thought about her
delicate and tender face. He could not understand how a person could
look death in the eye so many times and remain human, even be able
to smile and feel pity. But his hatred for the Nazis and his desire for
revenge impelled him to do this. Often he felt deep shame for being
German. He knew about the atrocities in the camps and often talked to
his friends about them in a low voice. But he was completely occupied
with the damned war of attrition on the Russian front, a war that only a
madman like Hitler could believe possible to win. He lost many of his
good friends and kept in touch with their families. Each day his doubts
grew about the sanity of the leaders of the Reich. He knew many thought
the way he did. Why did they obey blindly? "We Germans have been
blessed with a terrible curse: obediance," his father had told him before
he went to the front. "Some day it will lead to catastrophe." Again he

thought about the patient. Some inner drive compelled him to save her, no matter what. It was the only way to save his own soul.

He was so busy with his thoughts that he didn't notice the fear that gripped the people at the forester's house when they saw a German officer approaching. He handed them the letter and made signs indicating that he need women's clothes. The forester's wife quickly provided him with some. When he left they rubbed their eyes in surprise. They were still worried, and quickly delivered the letter to Mrs Fanger. Winczewic rushed into the forest and alerted Yankl Fanger. When Yankl finished reading the letter he muttered, "Traitor, she will turn all of us in. Stavinsky will pay for this with his life." He issued an order to bring Eju over. When the latter arrived, he read him the letter.

"Your sister is collaborating with the bloody Nazis. If we are caught you will be the first to die." He aimed his weapon at Eju's head. Eju started to cry and begged for his life. He asked for forgiveness and said he was not responsible for his sister's behavior, and that he was loyal to the group.

"What else do I have to do to prove it?" he asked, clinging to Fanger's boots. The latter hesistated when his mother started yelling and lashing him with her apron.

"Don't you see this doesn't make any sense? The boy is innocent. Don't touch him. Hannale will never betray us. Maybe it's a miracle. Maybe the German is really an angel who was sent to save us."

Yankl was surprised by the intensity of his mother's feelings and looked like an embarrassed child. Roleh stepped forward and put her arms around his neck, saying, "I knew you couldn't kill one of our own."

"To hell with you all," Yankl swore. "Not even a dog will be able to save you if we are caught."

He put down his weapon and told Eju to get up. "Come with me," he told his mother. "This place is no longer safe."

They went out cautiously and headed quickly into the woods. That night they changed their hiding place.

Hannale was transferred from the barn to another hiding place. It was a hut where they manufactured oil. A soldier was posted at the door with strict instructions not to let anyone inside. Because of the many rats scurrying about and Hannale's constant screams, she was transferred again to an abandoned farmer's house. Again a guard was assigned to her at Walter's command.

The roar of guns was getting closer. The local residents started fleeing, afraid of the approaching Russians. The German forces started their retreat. Hannale trembled in her room as she heard their commands. Deep inside she knew that the shelling was a blessing; the end of the nightmare was near. She didn't know whether she would enjoy the fruits of victory. She hoped that at least the forest dwellers would be saved. How relieved she was at the thought of her brother becoming free. She was afraid his need to avenge himself would drive him back to Glinyany, where his life would be in danger.

Her thoughts wandered back to Lvov. She remembered the school. Four years had passed since she had been forced to leave. How she longed to finish her studies. How she loved her books. She recalled Lvov's lovely buildings and green gardens. Would she ever see them again? She remembered Haim. She could not picture his face, but he seemed taller than ever before. He was sitting on his tank and giving orders on the radio. She felt herself running towards him like a mad woman, desperately shouting his name. Then she stumbled. With a supreme effort she was able to draw his attention. He stopped the tank, got off, and pressed her to his heart. He lifted her onto the tank and started racing madly. She lost her hold and fell. "Haim!" she cried, as she saw him disappear into the distance.

A loud explosion awoke her from her reverie. A shell had exploded nearby and the house shook as pieces of plaster fell on her head. Walter came in. He was dressed in spotted battle fatigues, a helmet, and a pistol. He looked somewhat threatening, and seemed to be in a hurry. But his face was soft and reassuring as he held her by her shoulders and said, "Listen, young lady, it is time to say goodbye. We are retreating from here this very moment. I cannot take you with me, but I am giving you a document that will help you. Show it whenever you are in danger." He started reading the letter: "I state that Ana Stavinska of Volhin worked in the kitchen of the First Panzer Division of the Wehrmacht after her husband was recruited by the Red Army. She should be allowed to reach volunteer camp in Germany. Signed, Walter Rosenkranz, Captain, Intelligence Officer, First Tank Division."

He handed her a military blanket and put a package wrapped in newspaper in her hand. "Food for the road," he whispered in her ear, kissing her on her forehead. She barely able to stop crying, she gripped his hand. Tears appeared in his eyes as he said, "When it's all over, please write to me. Remember my address: 25 Brunnen Strasse, Turringon. Don't worry, my child, God is with you."

He turned quickly to leave the room. Hannale remained frozen in her place, wrapped in her blanket yet feeling cold. She knew it would be better to wait till nightfall. She started fumbling in the package she had received and found a small bottle of cognac, chocolate and salami. It was a package for soldiers on the front. When it grew dark she slowly left the house and started marching quickly towards the woods. The roar of guns continued and the sky was it by flashes of gun fire. Her fear grew. She sat down in a trench the middle of the field. Suddenly she heard voices speaking Russian and she recognized that they were soldiers in Red Army uniforms. She felt like shouting and laughing hysterically. Everything was now behind her, and the nightmare was over. But suddenly she saw the black bands on their arms. "Vlasovchiks" (soldiers in the army of the Russian general Vlasov who fought on the German side), she whispered, alarmed. She tried to hide, but to no avail. They soon discovered her.

"Here is a little Jewess who is still alive," the sergeant said, pushing her rudely. They took her to their German main unit. Hannale was taken to a bunker. She faced a Wehrmacht officer, a mountain of a man in his late forties. His little eyes danced in their sockets and his red cheeks blazed when he was told in broken German that a Jewish girl had been found in the battle zone.

"The hell with you," he shouted. "The war is raging, the army is disintegrating, more people die every day and all you can think about is some miserable Jewish girl you happened to find. Get out of here and return to your post."

He turned to her and asked, "What about you?"

She was not afraid. She replied in perfect German, "They just started up with me."

He looked her over and blurted, "These Russian pigs."

He summoned a soldier and told him to attach Hannale to the Wehrmacht convoy retreating to Hungary. They put her in the back of a wagon, the driver of which turned out to be a Russian prisoner. Next to him sat a German soldier. The wagon was equipped with food supplies earmarked for the retreating soldiers. The convoy moved slowly and started climbing the Carpathian Mountains. Before dawn they passed a Ruthenian (belonging to a Slavic people living in the Carpathian mountains) village, where they were treated to sheep cheese. A muttering old Ruthenian farmer's wife blurted at Hannale, "who are you?"

"I am Polish, from the Volhin region. My husband was recruited by the Red Army and I worked in the kitchen for the German Army."

When the woman noticed that Hannale was wrapped in a blanket and wore torn clothes, she rushed into a house and came back with a village dress.

"Here, take it. God will be good to you."

When they resumed their journey the Russian prisoner whispered to her, "Whether you are Polish or not, you are lucky. I have never seen the Germans acting grateful to anyone."

On the third day of their journey they arrived at Unguar, near the border. Hannale's heart pounded as she recognized a large number of *mezuzot* on the doorposts of houses which were shut and bolted. There were many refugees in the town. Most of them were Ukrainians who had served the Germans faithfully and knew the war was about to be lost. Many of them were from Eastern Galicia, and Hannale was afraid someone might recognize her. She was given quarters in one of the local and only went out infrequently. Her task was to wait on a German officer.

One morning, when she brought him his shaving water and he started asking her about her past, and she stuck to her story speaking perfect German. The officer laughed and said, "Your husband is in the Red Army and we are retreating, but in the end the Third Reich will win. I am sure he is not alive and therefore would not object if I had a little fun with his wife."

She started stammering and asked permission to leave for a moment.

As she walked out he laughed and said, "Come back soon, my sweet."

When she got out of the house she started to run like a person possessed. Her feet carried her to the train station. She saw a line of people waiting patiently for the train. at the end of the railroad she saw a freight car and heard the neighing of horses. The sight of the beasts made her recoil. She recalled the *Aktion* in the ghetto and the stories of people jumping off cattle cars on the way to the extermination camps, and what they had gone through inside the train. She asked a young Ukrainian what was going on. He said, "These are volunteers who have signed up to escort this train and horses collected in Poland by the Wehmacht."

"Where are they going?"

"To Bishoftanitz."

"Where is that?"

"In Czechoslovakia," the young man responded. "We will be heading for a huge ranch."

She decided to join the train. Inside they were accommodated alongside the horses they had to feed. They were beautiful animals, bred on a ranch in Poland and confiscated by the Germans. At night the people slept on bags of straw. The horses kept sneezing and pounding the floor with their hooves. When the train passed a river they would fill huge tubs with water and serve it to the horses. On the train Hannale's attention was drawn to a seventeen-year-old girl with flax-colored hair and sad blue eyes. Her belly was swollen. From time to time the Ukrainians cursed her and spat in her direceton, muttering, "Dirty whore."

One evening Hannale turned to the girl and said, "Rumor has it you became pregnant by a German officer. I can see how much they are harassing you. Tell me, is it really true?"

The girl started to cry and said she had been raped by the German who had misled her. She had to flee her village to save her life.

"What is your name?" Hannale asked.

"Yulka Puchko," she said.

"And where are you going?"

"I am not sure. My brother volunteered for work in Austria two years ago, and he is now in Austria. I may join him."

"Listen," Hannale said, "I will help you. I know German well. I will protect you and you will say you are my cousin from Volhin."

Yulka burst into tears. She embraced Hannale.

"You're really going to help me?"

"Yes, don't worry. From now on we'll be together."

Most of the horse escorts were Ukrainian. They would pass green fields which seemed to have skipped the war. They also saw dozens of villages where life went on as usual. At one of the stops Hannale was approached by a young man who looked at her with a piercing stare, saying, "I'm told you are a Pole from Volhin. There are few Poles on this train. We don't believe you. Most likely you are a Jew."

Her blood froze, but she answered calmly, "I am Polish just like you. If you have any doubts you are free to complain."

"I will," he said and walked away. The next day Hannale was summoned by the German officer in charge of the train. She saw a man in his mid-sixties with graying hair and a thin, wrinkled face. His coat was too large. A cigarette dangled from the corner of his mouth. He looked drunk, and when he yawned one could smell liquor on his breath. Next to him stood a Polish woman in her mid-forties, who introduced herself as a physician. She was known to be the officer's mistress.

The doctor turned to Hannale and said in Polish, "There is a suspicion that you are Jewish. What do you have to say for yourself?"

Hannale ignored her, turning directly to the officer and saying in German, "I don't know what these people want from me. My name is Ana Stavinska. I am a Pole born and bred, and I have a letter to prove it."

She handed him Walter's letter. He snatched it and started to read. When he finished he said angrily, "What do I care who you are or what you are. This letter says you are worthy of our help. When we arrive at our destination they'll investigate. I have no time to check this matter. My job is to get this train safely to Bishoftnitz."

He slapped his mistress's behind and said, "Leave her alone," as he poured himself a glassful of brandy.

Hannale returned to her car unharmed, but she could not sleep. She knew the others had heard the suspicions against her and knew she was going to be investigated by the SS when they arrived at their destination. Everyone soon forgot the matter, but Hannale's heart beat quickly each time she saw the Polish physician.

The train stopped from time to time to water the horses in the river. Hannale and Yulka played in the water and splashed each other. Yulka's pregnancy was noticeable, and many of the passengers teased her, while others ignored her. Some even called her names.

"Hans promised nothing would happen to me," she reflected as she wiped away a tear, "he even hinted he might marry me when the baby was born. But where is he now? His unit was involved in the bloodiest battles with the Russians. Is he still alive? And why is everyone against me? After all, they have all collaborated with the Germans. All except for Ana. What an unusual woman, so different from the others, so kind-hearted." She had not met too many Jews, but from the rumors that spread in her village she knew they had met with a bitter fate. She did not understand the suspicions about Ana being Jewish, and was not at all bothered by them. She desperately needed someone who would support her during her ordeal. She was deathly afraid of giving birth. She clearly remembered the screams of the village women who were giving birth.

Ana met her expectations. Yulka argued that Ana was her cousin, although it seemed somewhat strange, since Yulka's hair was light and her eyes pale blue, while Ana's face, eyes and hair were dark, almost as dark as the gypsies' who sometimes stopped at her village. Who was this mysterious woman? She was not a the daughter of farmers. She did not have the coarseness and ignorance of the farm girls. Her manners were impeccable. She must come from the city, but from where? "Stop thinking these thoughts, Yulka," she rebuked herself. "She is your guardian angel, sent to you by the Holy Virgin." She crossed herself quickly and started wading again in the river. Together they carried the water-filled tubs to the train, watered the horses and quickly fell asleep on the bags of straw.

Hannale awoke. The animals stamped their feet and swayed from side to side. She watched a beautiful horse standing nearby. It returned a warm look, as if telling her not to worry. She could almost hear it whisper in Polish *Jakusz tubanzu* (somehow it will all work out). Hannale smiled and the beast sneezed again. It now looked at Yulka, who slept next to her. Her loud snores belied her great beauty.

The constant harassment they both suffered decreased considerably. The travelers felt the war was coming to an end and were concerned about their fate. Most of all they feared the Bolsheviks. They knew Germany was about to suffer a crushing defeat, but they hoped that the farther west they went, the better their chance to be saved. Most of them were Ukrainians. From their conversations Hannale understood that many of them had been active in the nationalist movement. She also learned that their hatred for the Jews was deeply rooted. Many bragged about killings and torture and seemed to blame all their troubles on the people of Israel.

"What have we done to them to deserve such hatred?" Hannale wondered. She remembered her father's words about the "return to Zion." The feeling of "redemption" overtook her, and she swore she would never rest until she fulfilled his and her own dream of setting foot on the land of their fathers. "Then we will have our revenge against these Amalekites. Oh, how sweet it will be!" In her mind's eyes she saw Moses standing on a high mountain with his hands lifted, looking over the battle with Amalek, Joshua bin Nun and Aaron at his side, supporting his hands. She suddenly became afraid his hands might drop and Amalek might win. She saw herself holding her father's hands and yelling at Eju, Please help me. Don't let go. Suddenly Aaron's hands fell and, in despair, he cried at his children, Run for your life. The battle is lost. Amalek won, Amalek won, Amalek won. . . .

Yulka stroked her forehead and whispered in her ear, "Anushka, you have typhus. You are hallucinating. I won't tell anyone. Don't worry."

Cold beads of perspiration covered Hannale's forehead. She looked deeply into Yulka's eyes and said, "You are not Amalek."

"Everything will be all right. You will recover." Yulka handed her some water.

Hannale stood up abruptly and said angrily, "I don't have typhus. I was only dozing."

Yulka begged her forgiveness for daring to mention that horrible disease. Finally they fell into each other's arms and embraced as Hannale repeated to herself, "This child cannot be Amalek."

The train stopped at Bishoftanitz. It was a breathtaking estate with a castle in the center, which the baron's family had used as its residence after fleeing the Germans. There was a beautiful valley and many stables next to a small pond. People came over to greet them, some out of curiosity; others were relatives who had arrived earlier. Hannale realized that she had to avoid any possible contact with the people staying at the castle, especially since some of them were from the vicinity of Glinyany and might recognize her. Hannale was put in a room with Yulka, apart from the rest. Once again her command of German helped her. The head of the kitchen was impressed with her intelligence and asked her to bring groceries from the next village. Each day she would ride her bicycle to the village store with a list of products. She made every effort to keep a low profile. When she rode she did not look left or right. Sometimes she could feel hostile eyes following her and when she got back to the kitchen she felt safe again. She knew deep down that she had to get out of Bishoftanitz before someone from the past identified her.

It was a cool morning. A light mist covered the ranch. Hannale put on her coat and started on her bicycle down the path to the village. On the side of the road stood a group of young Ukrainians on their way to work. Suddenly she heard a voice.

"Hanna! Hanna!" One young man broke out of the group and followed her, very excited. Her blood froze. She felt she was about to stop breathing, but she continued as if nothing had happened. When he finally reached her, she stopped her bicycle.

"My God, Hanna," he said, "you are the daughter of Aharon Hochberg and Munyu's sister. What are you doing here?"

"My name is Stavinska," she said and smiled. "I am from Vohlin. You are confusing me with someone else."

"I could swear it was you," he said and proceeded to swear in the name of all the Ukrainian saints.

"Goodbye," she said and resumed her ride. She kept going as if nothing had happened. When he disappeared she got off her bicycle and started running across the field as if possessed. It was Bunda, the son of their neighbor, Volodia, the farmer. He used to drive a coal wagon in

Glinyany. She had been so afraid this might happen, and yet she seemed to welcome it. "Won't it be better if I turn myself in?" she asked herself. "Isn't the peace of death better than the fear of death?"

She lay down on the weeds, covered with the dew of night. She tried to get up, but an inner voice ordered her not to move. She felt helpless. This young man would go to the police and turn her in. She did not remember him as an evil person, but she knew that the penalty for not turning in Jews was death. She knew he had not believed her story, since they had known each other as children, and people had sometimes suspected she was not Polish. All the evidence would be stacked up against her and she would be executed. Would Walter's letter save her? Oh, Walter, her only lifeline. Where was he? She slowly took out the crumpled letter. She knew it would not save her. She must write to him directly. She slowly stood up, mustering whatever strength she could find. She recalled that she had to bring some things back to the kitchen. She retraced her steps. "You mustn't lose your presence of mind, you mustn't get confused," she muttered.

On the way to her room she saw Yulka sewing. When she entered Yulka gave her a strange look. In her mind Hannale said to her, "So you, too, have found out I am Jewish. All right, turn me in, kill me!" She controlled herself and said, "I am very tired, Yulka. Please tell the kitchen head tomorrow that I didn't feel well and won't be reporting to work."

She sat down and wrote a letter to Walter at his home in Tiringen.

Dear Walter,
I am writing you in the hope that you are well and happy. I am in the village of Bishoftanitz in Czechoslovakia. I am doing volunteer work for the Wehrmacht. There is a young man here who thinks I am someone else and can cause me much trouble. No one knows me better than you, since you lived in our house in Pubituva in Vohlin. I would be most grateful to you if you could help me establish my identity.
                    Your friend,
                    Ana Stavinska

She knew she had to mention the fact that he had ostensibly stayed at her house in Vohlin, since the military censorship as well as the Gestapo opened foreign mail.

Hannale had several days of great fear. Finally she decided to go back to work. She noticed that the whispering about her had increased. Her fear grew daily; she felt the end was coming. Finally she received a letter from Walter's elderly father. He wrote that his son had not yet come back and was with his unit on the Russian front. He gave her the military mail address and wished her good luck in finding his son.

"This is it," Hannale thought. "I will never find him. He might have been killed, wounded or taken prisoner." Despite these depressing thoughts she wrote him, not expecting an answer.

A few days later, at noon, a policeman from the next village showed up at the estate, asking for Stavinska. Hannale heard the kitchen head call out, "Stavinska! Stavinska!" She opened her door and saw the gendarme. She had a bad feeling, yet at the same time she was relieved and went downstairs. She looked at the policeman without saying a word. She was ready to let him take her away when she heard his coarse voice booming, "Where is that Ukrainian pig who dared question your origin? I have a letter from Major Rosenkranz of the glorious First Panzer Division which confirms the fact that he was in your house in Vohlin during the retreat and that you are Ana Stavinska. Bring this boy at once."

They sent for Bunda, who was working in the field of one of the farmers who provided produce for the German army. Each farmer had a volunteer who did all the odd jobs. When he arrived the policemen took him by his arms and bent down his head.

"You are nothing but scum," he snarled and pushed him back. "What do you want from her?"

Hannale translated his words from German to Ukrainian. The young man started to shake and tried to mumble something in German. He turned to Hannale and said,

"Miss, I have nothing against you. Your resemblance to that girl might have confused me. Please tell him I have no ill intentions toward you."

A large crowd gathered around them. Hannale translated what Bunda had said for the policeman. When she finished he blurted angrily, "Tell this ignorant ass that if he keeps bothering you I'll send him to Yugoslavia to dig ditches."

The policeman left. Bunda mumbled some words of thanks and swore he would leave her alone. The crowd started to disperse and Hannale returned to her room. She felt relieved knowing that her credibility with the Germans as preserved. But she knew it was not over. The Ukrainians had been scorned. The rumor spread that, because of her, a policeman had been brought to the ranch and had insulted Bunda in front of everyone. They knew that a German officer had written a letter for her. When she rode her bicycle she would often hear people calling, "Dirty Polish whore. You left your husband and children for a German. You will end up giving birth to a bastard like that loose woman you live with."

When she passed in the street they would spit at her and curse. Life became unbearable, and finally Hannale decided to talk to the kitchen head. She said that Yulka was being harassed because of her pregnancy, and that the two of them wished to be sent to Knittelfeld in Austria, where Yulka's brother worked.

"You must understand, Stavinska, the situation is getting complicated. The trains these days are kept exclusively for the Wehrmacht. How will you get to Austria?"

"We will manage," Hannale said (almost adding in Yiddish, *Mit Got's help*). "You must help this poor girl. Don't forget the father of her child is a German. It doesn't matter where we work."

"Oh, well," the corpulent German murmured. He took out pen and paper and wrote:

To the Work Office in Knittelfeld, Paulo Morassati Company:
I hereby confirm that Ana Stavinska and Yulka Puchka work at the kitchen in Bishoftanitz under my supervision. They need suitable work.
Hans Werber, Kitchen Head

Hannale almost kissed him. She calmly took the letter and said quietly, "Thank you very much."

He pulled a wad of marks and food coupons out of his pocket.

"Here, take care of yourselves."

She quickly ran to see Yulka, who was sitting in her room knitting.

"Hurry, pack your things, we are leaving immediately and going to Knittelfeld, to your brother."

"What's the rush, please, why don't we leave tomorrow at dawn?"

"You don't have a moment to waste. Rumor has it that the Ukrainians are planning to disembowel you. Hans has arranged free passage cards for us."

Yulka shivered and started packing immediately. Within minutes the two were on their way to the train station. When they arrived at the station the place was buzzing with soldiers. She turned to the ticket clerk, showing him Hans's and Walter's letters.

"I'm sorry, you cannot board the train. We have instructions not to allow civilians on."

"This girl was impregnated by a German officer and she must run for her life," said Hannale, raising her voice.

"Impossible. These are my orders."

"What can I help you with, Fraulein?" came a voice behind her. When she turned she saw a short, thin officer. His face was attractive but stern.

"Lieutenant Johann Ditriech, Eleventh Infantry Division," he said clicking his boots and taking a polite bow.

"My name is Ana Stavinska, and this is my cousin, who is pregnant by a German officer. If we stay here her life will be in danger. I have letters of recommendation from important German officers."

After he had looked at her letters, he turned to the ticket clerk with a stern voice.

"These girls are an inseparable part of the Wehrmacht. You must arrange seats for them on the next train to Prague."

"Prague?" Hannale asked.

"Yes," he replied. "From there you continue to Vienna and Knittel-feld."

The train was loaded with German soldiers. Most of them looked tired and dispirited. Hannale hastened to relate that her cousin was carrying an Aryan child. They made room for them immediately and offered them food and drink, treating them with great respect. She now longer saw the young officer. Hannale listened to the complaint of the soldiers and recalled the caravan of wagons from Biala to Bishoftanitz. "They are almost children," she thought. "Are they aware of the atrocities their people have committed?" She had a sudden impulse. "Would they kill me if I told them I was Jewish; would they turn me over to the SS? Am I crazy? Where did I get such a crazy idea? I am trying to save myself, and yet I am tempting fate. Are they all cold-blooded murderers, or are some of them like Walter? Why not try? Hush," she silenced herself, "you must be mad."

She tried to catch their eyes, and some returned her look with a sad smile. For hours she thought she was about to lose her sanity and reveal her true identity to them. Finally she was overcome by fatigue and fell asleep. When she woke up they had arrived in Prague.

She had never been to Prague. Her father had always told her about the great beauty of the city, about the history of its Jewish community, and about its beautiful, ancient synagogue. Now it was a ghost town, empty and silent, defaced beyond recognition. "When I return home I'll tell father how disappointed I was," she thought absently.

Except for some military vehicles moving about, there was not a living soul in the city. Most of the stores were closed and shuttered. After a short, depressing stroll she returned to the train station.

Budapest was another world altogether. The street were full of pedestrians, and the city was clean and breathtaking. Well-dressed and made-up women strolled about, and the cafes were full. Hannale closed her eyes in disbelief. There were no people in military uniforms, and the stores were full of merchandise. The aroma of fresh baked goods reached her nostrils. She and Yulka walked about as if asleep. They entered an immaculate public bathroom. "Pangi, pangi," the old cleaning woman said to them. Hannale handed her a string of beads which the old woman grabbed, laughing, as she gave them a good portion of paper.

The vending girls giggled at the sight of the strange pair, a light-haired woman about to give birth and a dark one who looked like a gypsy dressed in rags. Finally they were told rudely to leave the store, and they resumed their walk as they munched on a tasty cake which Yulka had managed to take off the counter.

"Unbelievable," Hannale reflected. "Not only did the war fail to touch Budapest, but instead there is plenty and glitz everywhere." All the stately buildings stood intact. There was not the slightest hint of bombardment. The Danube was bluer than usual, and the influence of the Austro-Hungarian Empire could be felt. Hannale felt rage at all those people who had been spared the destruction, the suffering and the killing. "Why?" she asked. "Why are they so lucky not to have gone through a nightmare like mine, which refuses to end?"

She had a sense of outrageous injustice. She felt bitter and resentful. With eyes full of anger and envy she watched the spruced-up matrons around her. Yulka, however, was curious and full of wonder. She had never been to such a city before and it fired her childish imagination. She started humming a happy Polish folk song. On a street corner stood a man with a mustache kissing the hand of a young woman. Yulka burst out laughing and said to Hannale excitedly, "Look, Hans my lover will come back and kiss me again."

"Quiet," Hannale hissed angrily. "Don't you see it's all nonsense. These people have never suffered. There is no reason for us to feel happy for them."

Yulka looked at her in surprise and did not say a thing. Hannale realized she had gone too far and added gently, "I am sure Hans will look after you and the child. Come, let's return to the train station."

The journey to Vienna was short. When they reached the Austrian capital they immediately saw the ravages of war. Entire sections had been destroyed, and many houses have turned to rubble. They unboarded the train and got on a streetcar. The Czech inspector was friendly and let them travel the entire line and back. He told them almost every day Vienna was bombed from the air. Morale was low, and there was a terrible feeling of doom.

Pedestrians hurried along. Some stores and restaurants were open, but there were few customers. She recalled her parents' stories about this wondrous city, where they had spent their honeymoon in 1912. When her father came back from Vienna after his surgery he was full of praise about the miracles of medicine performed in that city. Now the place looked forlorn and pitiful. Here and there one could see remnants of the city's former beauty, like that of an old woman struggling to look presentable despite all the slings and arrows. Hannale did not feel an ounce of pity for the city. She knew that the Austrians were willing collaborators of the Nazis, with many active members of the Nazi Party. She was somewhat annoyed with her father, criticizing his naiveté regarding the true intentions and actions of this Aryan nation which he had praised so much. She kept asking herself how he could have failed to see the abysmal hatred of Jews? Did the halcyon days of the Austro-Hungarian monarchy or the magnanimity of Emperor Franz Josef mislead him and cause him to be so tragically wrong? But she forgave him. She could see how outward beauty and a rich culture could successfully cover up barbaric Germanic traits, capable of any atrocity. "It serves them right," she thought, "that they are learning what suffering means."

They had to spent the night at the Vienna train station. They were still waiting for a train for the journey to Steirmark, their destination. Finally they found one and the trip to the south continued. On the way Hannale could not help admiring the enchanting view of mountains, forests, brooks and small lakes. For the first time she traveled through long tunnels dug for the railroad. The magnificent view made her feel better, and thoughts of the approaching liberation and a brighter future took over.

When they reached Knittelfeld, in the Steirmark region, they walked over to the Paulo Morassati factory. They went immediately to the manager of the sawmill. Paulo Morassati was a rich Italian who owned many factories. In Knittelfeld he had a large sawmill which supplied a huge amount of lumber for the German and Italian armies. The local manager, Herr Kozzi, was a friendly, elderly Italian who spoke fluent German. Under him worked several junior managers, including Frau Primus, a fat, good-natured Austrian. Hannale and Yulka were assigned to her detail. They were housed in a spacious, clean hut. There were many workers there, most prisoners of war from other countries, with some volunteers. Among them was Andreas Puchko, Yulka's brother. They were told he was working outside the sawmill and would be back in the evening. In the meantime they were sent to the quartermaster to be fitted with work clothes.

When Hannale saw the clothes in the warehouse, she shivered. The sleeves of many of the coats were unraveled and their pockets torn off. Here and there she saw *tzitziot*, Jewish prayer shawls worn as part of a man's traditional garb. She knew these were the clothes of murdered Jews. The smell of the clothes was familiar. Tears welled up in her eyes, but she suppressed them and went out quickly. "I could have taken a garment belonging to my sister," she thought, as she marched quickly back to her hut. When they went to their room to wait for Andreas, she noticed that Yulka was becoming increasingly restless.

"What's the matter?" she asked.

"I'm afraid he'll kill me because of my pregnancy," she said.

"Don't tell him it was a German," Hannale cautioned her. "Tell him it was a Pole you met on the way."

Andreas Puchko was a young man in his twenties. He was tall and solid, and his face was broad and tanned. He had deepset blue eyes and his cheekbones protruded. His hair was blond like his sister's, carefully combed back. He wore the workclothes of the German army and brown leather boots. When he came in he greeted his sister but did not kiss her. Instead, he studied Hannale. Her hair was cut short, like a boy's, for fear of lice. She wore a skirt and a jacket which had been tailor-made for her from Walter's military blanket.

"Who is this important lady?" he asked Yulka.

"This is Ana. I met her on the way. She speaks German. If not for her I would not have made it. You know, Andreas, they bothered me because. . . ."

She checked herself and looked down. Suddenly he noticed her pregnancy. His face paled and there were beads of perspiration on his forehead. Hannale thought he was about to strike her.

"What is this?" he said angrily, pointing at her belly.

"It's not my fault," the girl started to whimper, "Hans promised to marry me."

"Hans, who is Hans?" His anger grew. Yulka threw herself on the bed and cried bitterly.

"Tell him, Ana. Tell him."

"You're a fool," Hannale told her, "I warned you not to tell him the truth."

She turned to Andreas.

"Hans is a German soldier of the Wehrmacht who forced Yulka. She was not able to resist, and there is no way of changing it right now. We must do everything we can to help Yulka."

"Damn," he muttered. "If people find out, I am lost." He made the two of them swear they wouldn't open their mouths.

"Oh, well," he said, "I'll find a father for your bastard."

Hannale joined the work force at the sawmill. She befriended some Austrian women who worked there and was often invited to their homes. Some of them added dresses they had made at work to her wardrobe, and life continued undisturbed.

One day Herr Kozzi turned to Hannale and said,

"Your cousin is about to give birth. Tell her we'll send her to the hospital in Gretz."

When she heard she was being sent to the hospital, Yulka started to cry. She did not want to go to a hospital. A hospital was a place where people died. She had never heard of a woman giving birth in a hospital. She ran away and hid and would not calm down until Hannale promised her she would not be taken to a hospital.

One evening Yulka started having birth pains but she did not say a word to anyone. Hannale returned to the hut and found her lying on the floor, writhing with pain.

"Help me," she screamed. Hannale panicked. She did not know the first thing about delivering a baby. She alerted one of her co-workers, who summoned a midwife. After a long night of suffering and fear, Yulka gave birth to a boy. It was a beautiful baby.

Hannale doted on the baby, oblivious to the man named Mikolai. This man made Hannale almost choke with fear. Her heart raced and her mouth would go dry. He was about forty five, short and broad-shouldered. His skin was dark like a gypsy's and his face was scarred. He had many tattoos on his body. He worked as a janitor and furnace lighter in one of the local schools. He said he had spent many years in

Beresa Kartuska, Poland's infamous jail. He had killed a woman in his village, for which he had received a life sentence. He claimed to have been drunk when he did it. When the Germans arrived the prison gates were opened wide and all the inmates dispersed. Mikolai agreed to take care of the mother and her child, and the next day Yulka moved in with him.

After Yulka left, Andreas started showing up more often in Hannale's hut. Sometimes he brought her flowers he had picked in the field, or a salami he had stolen from the kitchen. He became a devoted suitor. Since Hannale was not a coarse farm girl, he tried to be well-mannered, surprising himself by his own behavior. At first Hannale responded to him perhaps because she felt attracted to him or for fear she might cause trouble if she put him off. But when he announced he was moving in with her she was alarmed and told him it was impossible. He would not give up and continued with his desperate attempts.

Hannale decided to turn to his sister. She went to Yulka's hut. The crying of the baby could be heard through the window. She found the couple sitting next to the cradle. Yulka rocked the cradle and tried to calm the baby down and Mikolai was chewing tobacco and carving a piece of wood with his knife. He laughed derisively when he saw Hannale recoiling from him.

"Please, tell your brother I'm a married woman. I can't go on like this."

Yulka promised she would talk to him. Mikolai did not say a word and continued to carve with his knife, spitting on the floor from time to time. When she went to work the next day she noticed that Andreas had joined her group, but she did not say anything. Their job was to transfer beams which had become wet because of the snow to a dry place for storage. Suddenly a beam landed on Hannale's head. She grabbed her head and saw Andreas running quickly down the stairs of the warehouse and heading outside. This incident was repeated every day. He would drop a beam or a stump or put some obstacle in her way. Finally she went over to his hut and told him that if he did not stop she would complain to Herr Kozzi. This would create a scandal. She had to prevent this at all costs. She even considered letting him move into her hut; this would quiet his anger and everything would go back to normal. But she was deathly afraid of becoming intimate with him. Instinct told her what her cousin had said in the Przemislany ghetto: "The Gentiles smell the Jews and sense them nearby." Would Andreas find out she was Jewish if they lived together? This fear overcame all others; still she did not complain.

During a break Michel, a French prisoner, came over and asked her angrily, "Why do you let such a primitive barbarian taunt you without complaining?"

Michel was respected by everyone. He was a mechanical engineer and supervised the equipment at the sawmill. Herr Kozzi consulted him frequently, and when there was a problem with one of the machines Michel was the only one who knew how to repair it. He spoke perfect German and was quiet and polite, with small, delicate features, thin lips and a small mouth. His hair was dark brown and carefully groomed and his skin was pale. He always wore a pair of glasses. He never raised his voice.

Hannale was extremely surprised, but she said immediately, "No, Michel, you are wrong. He hasn't done anything to me."

Her answer made him even angrier, and he asked again, "Why are you afraid to talk to Herr Kozzi? I'll talk to him."

"No," Hannale pleaded, "please don't mention my name, don't complain."

Michel looked at her sternly, yet compassionately. They looked at each other for a while. That week Andreas was transferred to Yugoslavia to dig ditches.

Winter had almost passed, but the snow kept following in the Steirmark region. Spring was late in coming, and several work details made their way in the deep snow to the railroad, where they cleared the snow for the lumber trains that went to the main station in Knittelfeld. Hannale wore a pair of shoes with wooden soles she had received in the sawmill. She also had a pair of leather boots, but she hid them for fear the workers might take them away from her. One day, she wrapped her feet in rags and newspapers before putting on her wooden-soled shoes, but her feet froze and she fainted. She awoke in Herr Kozzi's office. her feet were soaking in a pail of warm water. Herr Kozzi looked concerned.

"Ana, I have a pair of boots I was given by the Red Cross. Wrap your feet and they will fit you."

Hannale thanks him profusely.

The two men took good care of her and saved her legs from amputation. Michel would bring her special food and German newspapers. Once when they were alone he whispered to her, "The Germans are having great trouble in Stalingrad. The war should be over soon."

On New Year's Eve she missed the dance at the sawmill, saying she was not feeling well. Michel did not go either.

The air raids intensified. The Allies attacked Knittelfeld with a fury because of the presence of a local tool factory that had been converted into an armory. The area was bombed every day. Danger was growing and the warnings they received did not allow them to reach the bomb shelter. At times they had to run and hide in the surrounding hills, where they found shelter under the trees. Most of the woods dwellers stayed in the woods and were afraid to return to their homes.

"Let them go to hell," Hannale thought and felt vindicated.

When she recalled the long and exhausting period she had spent in the Yachtorow forest in order to survive, she did not feel any pity for them. She felt pity for Yulka's baby. Mikolai forbade her to take the baby into hiding during the bombings. When the bombing stopped Hannale would run to Yulka's barracks. Furniture fell, windows were smashed, but the infant was not harmed. This happened with every air raid. Finally Hannale could not stand it any longer and fumed at Yulka, "Well, Mikolai forbade you to baptize him, but why do you agree to leave him here in such mortal danger?"

A few days later, when they had to run again, she saw Yulka carrying the baby with her as Mikolai limped behind. Some time later Yulka surprised her by saying, "I would like you to be my son's *matka chrzestna* (godmother)."

She asked a friend of her brother's to be the godfather. The latter turned to Ana one evening and said, smiling, "You know what, Ana, you look exactly like a Jewish girl I knew in the Krakow ghetto."

"Yes," Hannale said calmly, "you are not the first to mention this. It seems that not all of us are blond."

What worried her the most was the baptism ceremony. She had never taken part in a Christian ritual. Although Jews, Poles and Ukrainians lived next to one another in Poland, they knew nothing about the other's religion. She could not fall asleep. This was a critical test for her. She lay in bed and kept crossing herself, hoping she was doing it right.

"God," she asked, "why didn't you give me time to become a Christian? It all happened so fast. Who will help me?"

In the morning Knittelfeld came under heavy bombardment by the Allies. The church was wiped out. Hannale felt greatly relieved, but not for long. The priest decided to baptize the baby no matter what. He invited the party to his house. Hannale felt like a convict on death row, whose sentence had been commuted and was now reinstated. This time she was less afraid and decided to take the plunge. The tension and fear of being discovered had become unbearable.

Yulka held the baby as the priest dipped his fingers in the holy water and passed them over the baby's head, making the sign of the cross. He sprayed water on the baby's head and started to pray. Hannale began to murmur after him. Suddenly the priest handed her the baby. She held him with trembling hands and kept mumbling frozen in place when the godfather came over and stretched his hands toward her. She handed him the baby and the party walked outside, where Hannale and Yulka kissed each other.

"Thank you," she said. "If not for you, this child would never have been baptized. You are my son's baptizing mother and I shall never forget it."

Hannale was engulfed by an absurd feeling of victory. She felt a kind of euphoria and started shaking the hands of the guests with genuine feeling. She even surprised Mikolai with an embrace. She felt that the angel of death had lost this round, and now she was prepared for anything.

The winter continued, and the weather refused to change. Hannale and Michel would run for their lives during each air raid using Michel's bicycle. There were prisoners of many nationalities there—French, English, Yugoslav, Italian (from the army of General Badolio, which had rebelled against Mussolini), and Russian. Most were given in easy tasks, but not the Russians. Most of the prisoners were visited by the Red Cross and, except the Russians, would sometimes receive various goods. From time to time a festive dinner would take place and all were invited. There were no humiliations, and all were treated fairly by the Germans, except for the Russians. Hannale and Michel noticed that the latter were treated like animals. They were given the most difficult tasks, their food was meager, and they wore rags. They were given no medical attention. They were beaten savagely and were often shot to death for the slightest reason. Hannale, who understood their language, saw that their morale was extremely low. They were bent over, unlike the English, who behaved like nobility.

One day, as Hannale's group pushed the lumber cars to the train station in town, they passed a group of Russian prisoners busy loading wood on the large cars. Suddenly a group of German guards started beating a Russian prisoner with their rifle butts; he fell down, writhing in pain. His friend, who stood nearby, spat contemptuously and was shot to death on the spot. Hannale held on to the car and felt she was about to pass out. She became nauseous and was filled with hatred for the Germans. Memories from the ghetto, the woods, her parents' and sister's deaths agitated her, but some weakness prevented her from running over to the loading area, snatch the gun of one of the guards and shoot the Germans indiscriminately. Her fists were clenched but she felt helpless. She started to cry but no one noticed her. When she returned to the camp she entered Michel's hut and screamed, "I can't take it any more, Michel. Why are they doing it? You must do something, Michel. Don't let them kill Russians.

Michel calmed her down and told her he too was bitter, but as a prisoner it was unlikely he could do anything about it. Even if he spoke to Herr Kozzi, it would have no effect on the German guard.

"Poor souls," he said. "They have nowhere to go. The Germans kill them mercilessly, but if they go back to Stalin, their fate is death because they are not allowed to let themselves be taken prisoner. In the Red Army you are expected to fight to the end."

Most of the Ukrainians and Poles argued that the Russians deserved such treatment, and were being paid back for oppressing other nationalities in their own country. Hannale did not accept this view.

She liked the Russians. Not only were they good people, but they were also the only nation that had offered a haven to Jews, and those who had taken advantage of it before the Germans arrived were saved.

"When the war is over they will pay an unbelievable price," said Michel. "These criminals will pay for everything."

A sweet sensation enveloped her. "Revenge," her mother had commanded.

"I wish you could have met her," she murmured.

"Met whom?" Michel asked.

She was embarrassed. After a moment's confusion, she said quickly, "Nothing, no one. . . ."

The snow began to melt. One could see patches of green. The sun peeked occasionally, and everyone would start removing their warm winter clothes. Life seemed to continue as usual, but the bombardments increased in intensity. The sound of cannons came closer and closer, and there were signs of worry on the faces of the German guards. They knew the Russians were closing in and the Wehrmacht was about to collapse. The torturing of Russian prisoners subsided somewhat. From time to time a camp guard would disappear and rumor would have it that he had deserted.

Tension was highest the Ukrainians. Anything other than a German victory would mean disaster for them. Many knew that if they fell into the hands of the Russians they could expect a bitter fate. One could hear them whisper about running west, and many escape plans were discussed. Hannale took ill. Her temperature rose and she was cold. She became extremely weak and had to lie down. Michel rushed to see Herr Kozzi.

"Ana Stavinska is ill. We must transfer her immediately to the hospital."

"Hospital? What hospital?" Herr Kozzi fumed. "Knittelfeld and its hospital have been bombcd and are lying in ruins. There is no transportation. Food supplies are running out and the Russian are closing in."

"She will die, Herr Kozzi. Isn't there any other way?" Michel asked with a pained voice.

"As far as I know, the hospital at Gretz was also destroyed. The only remaining place is Vienna. How the hell do you expect to get her there, Michel?"

"The food supply truck is still running. Give me a travel pass. I'll take Ana to Vienna and come back with some provisions."

"My head is on the line if anything happens to this truck. You must return immediately to Knittelfeld after you bring Ana to the hospital. Here are the keys and the travel pass. I don't believe they will give you any provisions in Vienna, but try your luck. My God be with you."

They departed immediately. Ana lay in the back; her temperature rose and she started hallucinating. Michel drove fast, dodging the many craters formed by the repeated bombings. From time to time the truck would jerk and Hannale was thrown. There were not too many road blocks. Entire villages had been abandoned, and their domestic animals roamed about freely. Signs of defeat were in evidence. In the schoolyard one could see boys dressed in Hitler Jugend uniforms marching with wooden rifles on their shoulder.

"How sweet revenge will be," Michel thought to himself, imagining himself settling accounts with the Nazis. "I will be the commander of a firing squad that will liquidate these SS bastards. No, I'll interrogate them instead and torture them in their own cellars." He was overcome by hatred, and for a moment he forgot the purpose of his trip. But when he heard Hannale's moaning, he stopped the truck, rushed to the back, wet a towel in a puddle and put it on her feverish forehead. On the outskirts of Vienna they stopped at a military road block. Their papers were checked somewhat perfunctorily by the guard, who warned them the city was bombed daily from the air and the food supplies were dwindling, not to mention medication. He gave them some crackers and wished them a safe trip.

When they reached the hospital for foreigners, Hannale was put on a stretcher and laid down on the floor in one of the corridors. She still had a high temperature and her hallucinations continued. When she woke up she was bathed in sweat and still shivering from cold. She was alone in a room with whitewashed walls and a small cross hanging on the wall. A tall man entered the room. He had thick eyebrows and brown hair, and seemed to be in his forties. His face was pale and solemn.

"My name is Dr. Stanislaw Kuszinski," he said in perfect Polish. "I am the official doctor of the hospital for foreigners. You are quite ill, but

I believe you will improve. By the way, we don't have any medication here, but don't worry. I will personally look after you."

Hannale felt reassured. She lay there, spent, and looked at this man. His voice was soft and caressing. His eyes smiled as if hiding a secret. His features seemed Semitic, but his pale skin and perfect Polish belied that impression.

"Are you. . . ?" She cut herself short. She was excited and started to tremble.

He put his hand on her head, stroked it and said,

"Don't be upset, young lady. Everything will be all right. Here, drink some water."

He handed her water from the jar at the head of the bed. Hannale took some and lay back as she continued to look at him. He took a chair and sat next to her. There was deep silence and she fell asleep again.

A few days went by and Hannale began to recover. Her fever dropped and she regained her appetite. Dr. Kuszinski told her she was ready to go back to Knittelfeld. When she mounted the truck she noticed that Michel had become impatient.

"Hurry up," he urged her, "the situation is extremely grave. There is total anarchy in Knittelfeld. I tried hard to convince Herr Kozzi to let me take the truck. Now the roads are under fire and the Russians are approaching. I'm not even sure we'll be able to reach Knittelfeld."

The truck hurried along and Hannale managed to wave goodbye to Dr. Kuszinski through the window, as he blew her a kiss.

"See you after the war," she heard his voice from behind.

"After the war, after the war," an echo replied. "Is such a thing possible?" she wondered.

Michel stopped for fuel. From time to time he had to get off the main highway and take side roads. On the way they passed many Wehrmacht convoys heading west. No one asked them for their destination. The faces of the soldiers were droopy and many were wounded. Michel spat whenever he saw a column retreating. Hannale felt a certain sadness. She looked closely at the officers, trying to find Walter. She barely restrained herself from shouting when she thought she had seen him. When they reached Knittelfeld the camp was surrounded by darkness and there was an eerie quiet. They had to feel their way in the dark. No guards were seen when they reached the residential area. They noticed great activity, especially among the Ukrainians. Several people came out of their barracks, hastily carrying their belongings. They seemed eager to be on their way. Suddenly Hannale saw Yulka with her child. She ran up to her.

"What is going on?" she asked in alarm.

"Don't you know? Germany has surrendered."

Hannale felt her head spin. Michel had to stop her from falling. The air seemed to leave her body.

"Impossible," she told Yulka. "It must be a rumor spread by the Ukrainians."

When the news was translated for Michel, he started dancing and jumping for joy. Hannale was startled .

"Hush," she said, "there is still danger."

She did not close an eye all night. This was not how she had imagined the war would end. It was only a blind guess on Yulka's part. She had expected a liberating army to march through, with many flowers and balloons flying in the air. "Such a terrible war cannot end just like this. Where is the aura of victory? Where is the joy? Where is vengeance for the murdered?"

When dawn rose she got up and got dressed quickly. There was total chaos in the streets of Knittelfeld. Posters pasted throughout the city said, *"Deutchland Hat Capitulir"* (Germany has capitulated). Admiral Doenitz had signed the surrender. Horse-drawn wagons were carrying families and their belongings west. There were rumors that most of the collaborators were running for their lives. There were also rumors that the Knittelfeld butcher had fled to the mountains. His first wife had been a converted Jew; when the Nazis took power he decided to divorce her and she had been taken to a concentration camp. The old Austrian women argued that he had committed a despicable act and would have to pay for it.

They said the Russian army was a few hours from Knittelfeld. There was no joy. No flags were flown, and there were no shouts of victory. Even the feelings of revenge were somewhat blunted. Hannale returned to the sawmill. She felt satisfaction at the thought of now being able to go back to Glinyany. She would go and look for her brother. She was glad the Russians would liberate her. She tried to imagine what they would look like. Would they come by tanks or on foot? Would their uniforms look like Haim's? Would they wear boots?

Many of the labor camp residents fled when the guards left their posts. Only a small number of workers and prisoners remained. The next day the Russians arrived at the sawmill. Everyone remained locked in the barracks. There were orders in Russian telling them to come out. A small group of soldiers stood by, looking curiously at the emerging people.

"Does anyone here speak Russian?" they asked. Hannale stepped forward and smiled.

"I speak Russian and German," she said.

"What's your name?" the officer asked.

"Ana Stavinska," she replied. "I am from Vohlin, and I was recruited for labor after my husband was drafted by the Red Army."

"Who are the people in the camp?"

"Besides forced labor, there are some prisoners from other countries."

"Are there any Russian prisoners?" he asked angrily.

"No," Hannale replied, "as far as I know. Most of them ran away for fear of their own army. They knew what would happen to them if their surrender to the Germans was discovered."

"Traitors," he hissed and spat on the ground. He then softened down and said, "Life's routine will continue. You don't have to work any longer. Tomorrow we'll start identifying all the residents of the camp. Try to limit yourselves in your food consumption. The Red Army cannot supply you with all your needs, since our own food is dwindling."

Hannale and Michel went to town to try to find some food. Hannale walked around for several hours until she noticed a Russian soldier following her. When she returned to the camp he tried to catch up with her and said,

"I speak some German. Can you help me?"

Her heart beat furiously; he spoke Yiddish. She felt hot and began to sweat.

"Please," she said in German. "How can I help you?" She couldn't stop trembling.

"Tell me, are there any Jews here? I would like to help them."

"Jews?" Hannale breathed heavily. "There are no Jews. They no longer exist. They were all exterminated, murdered." She looked down and continued in German, "I don't believe you're going to find any Jews."

He did not seem at all surprised by her answer, and said, "Yes, I am sorry to say this is what I have experienced along the way."

He turned to leave. Hannale ran back to her room, fell on the bed and started to cry.

"Why didn't I tell him I was Jewish? Why didn't I speak to him in Yiddish? Why didn't I embrace him? Why am I still afraid?" she yelled, pounding the table with her fists. After a while she calmed down. There was food in her basket. She ate, completing her meal with a juicy red apple. She decided to reveal her Jewish identity the next day and ask for permission to go back to Glinyany. After much hesitation she got up her courage and approached the officer.

"Hello, comrade," he said. "So, how is life under the rule of the glorious Red Army?"

"Everything is fine," she smiled. "In fact I am. . . ."

"What do you say about our tremendous victory against these stinking Nazis?"

"Bless Stalin," Hannale replied. "I'd like to say that. . . ."

"You know," he interrupted again, "they did one smart thing I am happy about."

"What's that?" Hannale asked and her voice started to tremble.

"They got rid of the Jews. Finally we are done with them."

Hannale turned around and started running back to her barracks. She did not hear the officer chuckle as he said,

"Another one who feels sorry for the Jews."

She fell down. When Michel picked her up he could hear her murmur, "Bastards, my father was right. How could I believe them?"

Michel tried to calm her down. He did not ask her why she was upset. Finally she said, "The British are on the other side of the river in Judenburg. I would like to go over to their zone. Would you come with me?"

"Yes," he said.

After a few days she was summoned to the camp office. There she was surprised to see Dr. Stanislaw Kuszinski sitting comfortably and chatting with the Russian officer.

"Doctor," she said respectfully in Polish, "what brings you here?"

"Well," he said, "would you like to join me for a short walk?"

They went outside. Hannale took his arm and whispered, "Good to see you. Please tell me about yourself."

"Well," he said, "I studied medicine in France. I practiced medicine in Warsaw until the German occupation and was then transferred to Vienna to the hospital for foreigners, where you were hospitalized for pneumonia. You probably don't remember," he said jokingly, "but wet sheets saved your life."

They kept walking. Hannale took hold of him and said, "I'll tell you something, but you must swear on what is most precious to you that you won't tell anyone."

She fell silent.

"Are you pregnant?" he asked. "Are you suffering from some disease? Tell me."

She waved her hand.

"No, that is not it. I am Jewish."

She was seized by a sudden fear. She let go of him and stopped walking. She noticed that he did not get excited, but continued to walk slowly.

"Did you hear what I said?"

"Yes, I know," he said.

"What?" she cried. "How?" A wonderful feeling of freedom pervaded her. He stopped and smiled.

"Only a Jewish girl would say, *Mameh, mameh, ich starb avek* (in Yiddish: Mother, mother, I am dying) when she hallucinates."

Hannale burst out laughing.

"You knew all along, you knew all along."

Dr. Kuszinski grew serious and said, "Now I'll tell you something, but you must swear on what is most precious to you to guard it."

"You can trust me."

"I am not a doctor. My name is Yosef Singer, from Lublin. Before the war I worked as a pharmacist. My wife and two children were taken away and I was hidden by the pharmacy owner. After the Warsaw Ghetto uprising the pharmacist suggested that I join the fighters who surrendered and were sent to forced labor camp in Austria and Germany. I told them I was a doctor and I was sent to the hospital in Vienna. As I told you, when you hallucinated you revealed your origin, and I had to isolate you. After the liberation I remembered you were in Knittelfeld and this is why I came here."

"I'll never leave you," Hannale said as emotion filled her. He pressed her to his heart and they continued to walk.

The next day, after dark, a group of refugees crossed the bridge to Judenburg. Hannale, Michel and Yosef Singer were joined by Yulka, Mikolai and Andreas, who had returned from Yugoslavia. When they reached the British side they were grouped with other refugees and given quarters in a schoolhouse. Much to her disappointment, Hannale identified some Ukrainians whom she knew to be hostile. The refugees were dressed in khaki uniforms and military shoes supplied by the British. Hannale noticed the difference in atmosphere, which was much more relaxed on this side; the Russian side was filled with constant tension and suspicion. Food was plentiful. The British even tried to organize singing and drama events for the refugees.

One morning Yosef Singer turned to Hannale and said, "My dear, I must go to Lublin to find someone who can tell me what happened to my wife and two children. Wait for me here, I'll be back. I promise you I'll be back."

Tears flooded Hannale's eyes.

"Go safely and come back safely," she said and kissed him.

Rumors circulated in Judenberg about refugees of various nationalities waiting in Italy. It was said that help was given to locate relatives. In the British zone there was no limitation on crossing the border. Michel decided to try his luck. His farewell from Hannale was wrenching. When he departed, Hannale was left with Yulka and her men. She felt alone again and her thoughts wandered back to her native town of Glinyany. She started thinking about Eju. The fact that she hadn't seen her brother Munyu since the start of the war bothered her all the time. She wrote a letter in Polish and Hebrew:

My name is Hannah Hochberg and I am the daughter of Aharon Hochberg of Glinyany. I am looking for my brothers Eju and Munyu Hochberg and my brother-in-law Anshel Dresner.

She gave the letter to a young man named Boris who was going to Italy to find his fortune. When Boris crossed the border he ran into some British soldiers. They asked for his identity and, since he did not speak English, they searched him and found Hannale's letter.

"Damn it," the sergeant fumed, "I can't read a single word. The writing reminds me of Palestinian writing."

He summoned Tzvi Buchbinder, who was from Palestine. Tzvi was having a long conversation with the chaplain of the unit, Rabbi Solomon of Manchester. The rabbi was tall and blond, his curly hair disheveled, his face flushed, and his shirt open. He wore the uniform of the British Army and had a patch on his sleeve with the blue and white flag. When he started reading Hannale's letter he shivered. "The daughter of Aharon Hochberg," he mumbled to himself trying to control his emotions. He choked with tears. The men around him asked what was the matter.

"What do you know," he said, "the daughter of my father's best friend was saved. Unbelievable, unbelievable."

Rabbi Solomon immediately ordered a military jeep and the two drove to Judenburg. When they arrived they were told the refugees had been transferred to a camp in Innsbruck. There they were housed in a breath taking resort and enjoyed excellent weather. Hannale and Yulka sat on the bank of a lake in their bathing suits, which they had sewn for themselves. Suddenly they heard an announcement on the loudspeaker: "Hannah Hochberg is being summoned by the camp commandant." Hannale froze. The announcement was repeated. Hannale started breathing heavily and was seized again by a feeling of helplessness and the thought that the end had come.

"Who has revealed my secret?" she stammered in Yiddish and started to shiver. Yulka looked at her incredulously. "Ana, what's the matter? Aren't you feeling well?"

Hannale rose slowly and started trudging towards the office. Where were the SS? Where were the Ukrainians? Were they conspiring with the British? Here was proof that Germany had not surrendered and that all that had been taking place in recent weeks was a German plot. Run away! Run while you can! Have you gone mad? After all you've been through you're going to turn yourself in? Will you be taken like a sheep to slaughter? With these thoughts racing through her head she continued toward the group of people huddling near the camp headquarters. When she reached them she stopped and looked at a redheaded young man who asked her in Hebrew,

"Hannah Hochberg?"

Suddenly she saw a flag with the Star of David and two blue stripes. It looked familiar, yet totally different from the one she had known in her youth, the precious flag her father had given her for her twelfth birthday. Suddenly she roared in Hebrew, "Who are you, who are you?"

"Tzvi Buchbinder," the young man said. "My father is Asher Corech"

She threw her arms around him and clung to him with all her might. Tears streamed down her face. Rabbi Solomon started to sob, while all the camp residents stood around and applauded as they huddled together. Yulka came over and said, "I swear to you, Ana, I've known all along you were Jewish, but I didn't tell anyone."

"Thank you," Hannale whispered and started to relax. She told her story to Tzvi and the rabbi. A beautiful woman, about thirty, with straw-light hair and green eyes turned to Tzvi. She had two children with her who looked perfectly Aryan. She circled him and pointed at the flag sewn on his uniform.

"What is this?" asked Eva, known to all as a refugee of Latvian origin, whose husband had served in the Wehrmacht.

"This is the flag of Israel," Tzvi replied proudly, showing his shoulder to everyone around him.

"Are you a Jew from Israel?" Eva asked innocently.

"Yes," Tzvi replied, "from Jerusalem." Hannale translated his words.

"Aah," said Eva and kept circling him. Suddenly she started sobbing, and cried out in Yiddish, "My name is Fania Rosenfeld and I have two brothers in Rehovot. Please save me, take me and my children to the land of Israel, I beg of you."

"You, Eva, are a Jew?" Hannale asked, amazed. "How did you save two circumcised children?"

With their few belongings and great hope in their heart, Hannale, Fania and the two children were let on the jeep and rode to Udine, in the Friuli region in northern Italy. On the way Tzvi tried to explain Hannale's pedigree to the rabbi.

"My father had been sent to Eretz Yisrael on the recommendation of Aharon Hochberg. After he settled in Jerusalem, the two of them kept writing to each other in the holy tongue. Without Aharon's recommendation my father would not have received a visa. Do you know what a learned man he was? He was versed in the Torah and in both the Babylonian and Palestinian Talmuds. Everyone praised him, and his speeches were full of the fire of Torah and all the holy books."

Tzvi made sure the flag of Israel flew atop the jeep's antenna wherever he went, as he did now. They drove through the streets of an Italian village as a group of refugees waved to them. Suddenly he came to a screeching stop. On the road in front of them lay a woman who looked like a local resident.

"*Shma yisrael adonai eloheinu adonai ehad,*" she started crying, and grabbed the front wheel of the jeep.

"Who are you?" Tzvi asked after he got off the jeep.

"*Shma yisrael,*" she kept repeating over and over again.

Hannale got off, stroked her head and said softly, "I know what you have gone through and what you feel right now. What is your name?"

"Marilka," she said.

"Marilka what?"

"Marilka, that's all."

And so Marilka, a Jewish refugee from Poland, who had spent the entire war in a peasant's cellar without ever coming out, joined their party.

The group arrived at a camp organized by Yehezkel from Kfar Yehezkel. They were put into crowded tents. Every night they would stay up and sing songs of Israel. They would dance the *hora* around the camp fire and dream of living in Israel. Yehezkel, a husky young man of about forty, would keep lifting their spirits.

"We are waiting for certificates from the British," he said. "Don't worry. Everything will be all right."

It was Friday. Welcoming the Sabbath, Hannale said the blessing over the candles.

"*Baruch atah adonai eloheinu melech haolam asher kidshanu b'mitzvotav v'tzivanu ladlik ner shel shabbat.*"

"Amen," the crowd responded. Yehezkel was moved and wiped away a tear. It was not proper for a man to cry. A moment later he spoke.

"We did not know how terrible it was. We did not know about Auschwitz. We did not know about Babi Yar (a forest in Rusia which was a large killing ground of Jews)."

From Udine they went to Milan. They were housed at Via Unione 5. There Hannale wrote her name on the schoolhouse wall in big Hebrew letters. From there they were taken to Naples, where they received their certificates for Palestine. In Naples they were housed at an insane asylum that had been converted into a transition camp for refugees. They were taken to the harbor, where people of many nationalities awaiting repatriation were waiting. Hannale was waiting to board the ship. She saw French refugees marching and singing the Marseillaise. She jumped up as if she had been bitten by a snake.

"Michel, Michel!" she cried. Michel turned his head. The two ran towards each other. They stood there for a long silent moment embracing each other. Finally she said, "Michel, I am a Jew. My name is Hannah, not Ana. I am going to Palestine, to my land of Israel."

"Yes, I know," Michel said. "Your Polish friends made sure I knew. I have a surprise for you. I am also a Jew. Michel Baum. A Jew, you hear? All my prisoner friends kept the secret the whole time. No one turned me in. I owe my life to them. I'm going back to Lyon to look for my fiancee, Chantelle. Who knows if she is still alive."

The two said goodbye. Each turned to his or her own ship. Hannale went on board the ship. As she went up she turned her head towards Naples bay. She was taken with the rows of palms she saw everywhere. She was enchanted by the blue sea and the small, white-capped waves. Most of the refugees were put on the deck of this ragtag ship. A deafening whistle was heard and the ship began to plow its way into the sea. For several days they watched the horizon, hoping to see the shores of the promised land. One morning, as the sun was high in the sky and its brightness was blinding the few refugees who were not asleep, while the mothers held their children in their arms, Marilka's voice suddenly called, "Hannale,

Hannale, get up quick, see the shores of Eretz Yisrael in the distance."

Because of the sun they could barely make out a narrow strip of land on the horizon. But they were all gripped by great excitement. Everyone crowded on one side of the ship, making it tilt from the weight. The captain had a hard time steering the ship and preventing it from capsizing. Many broke into song and joined arms in a spirited *hora* dance. The joy was boundless.

A British destroyer approached the refugee ship and ordered it to stop. Several soldiers boarded the ship and asked for the passengers' papers, which they checked closely. After they were done they ordered the ship to follow the battleship to the Haifa harbor.

When they approached Haifa, Hannale looked wide-eyed at this Hebrew city which had never come up in her father's tales. It did not even belong to the kingdom of David. But there was something magical about the city. A breathtaking bay reminded her of the Bay of Naples. White houses with red roofs were surrounded by green vegetation. There was a graceful calm about this place. It was love at first sight. For a long time she stood there and watched, until they reached the pier, which was full of people. There were soldiers with rifles and bayonets, together with perspiring men in light suits, members of the Jewish Agency. The men on shore had dark skin, like the men in Naples, but their clothes were different. They wore gowns and strange headdresses made of cloth. Many had thick mustaches and frightening expressions. Hannale felt some hostility toward the newcomers. Some of them , upon reaching the shore, bent down and kissed the soil of the holy land. But the hostile atmosphere and the calls of the soldiers to advance to a single place cast a shadow over them.

Hannale walked slowly towards the harbor terminal and looked around with growing curiosity.

"Hannah, Hannah!" she heard someone call out. It was her cousin, Bruria, daughter of Israel Hochberg, the owner of the bank in Glinyany. She hadn't changed a bit. She was short and round. In her youth she had joined the Hashomer Hatzair, against her uncle Aharon's wishes. She went to farm training near Glinyany and emigrated to the land of Israel before the war broke out.

"This is training for lechery and abomination," Aharon used to rail. Bruria married a good-looking young man who had worked in her father's bank in Glinyany. They joined the Bet Oren *kibbutz* on Mount Carmel and began to fulfil the socialist dream. When Hannale recalled her aunt, Bruria's mother, Bella Rivka, she broke into a wide smile. Unlike her own mother, Rivka, whose cleverness was praised by all, her aunt was a short, fragile woman with a hook nose and stern face who often incurred the wrath of those who did not wish to listen to her criticisms.

Bruria strongly resembled her mother, but unlike her mother she was an easygoing, friendly soul. After the formalities at the harbor, they were finally able to embrace each other. Their hearts' floodgates burst open and they both started speaking at the same time, telling each other all they had been through, hardly hearing each other. Finally she decided Bruria would come to visit Hannale in a few days at the temporary detention camp in Atlit, south of Haifa.

After the authorities pronounced them healthy, they were allowed to join their relatives. Hannale was taken by a truck loaded with vegetables, driven by Benyu Shahaf. They drove up Mount Carmel through breath-taking pine groves and fruit orchards. The sea receded into the distance but they could still see the white-capped waves crashing against the walls of the Crusader castle on the Atlit shore. The rows of palm trees and the banana plantations at the feet of Mount Carmel lent the scene an exotic aura. Hannale had never been to a kibbutz before. When they arrived at the gates of the village they saw small white houses with red tiled roofs scattered inside deciduous groves.

They found the atmosphere at the kibbutz friendly and pleasant. Hannale moved in with Bruria and Benyu and it was decided to assign her to the kindergarten to help care for the children. She took to the tiny tots, who soon taught her "everyday Hebrew," so different from the classical Hebrew she had been taught. She enjoyed the little pranks the *sabras*, or natives of the land of Israel, played on one another.

Hannale decided to pursue the study of educational methods. To achieve this goal she had to join the *kibbutz* school at Yagur. She left Bet Oren with a heavy heart, separating again from her relatives and the children she had grown attached to. In Yagur she submitted her curriculum vitae. To her great surprise she was informed by the principal that she had to improve her Hebrew. She used the little money she had earned from her work in the kitchen to pay the tuition. She shared her room with Tip and Hedva, two native daughters of the *kibbutz*. She objected to the casual relationships that prevailed at the *kibbutz*. She put off the young men with the excuse that she was too busy with her studies, which happened to be true.

Hannale was invited to visit her cousin, Shalom Graff, and his wife Devora in Jerusalem. She was very excited. The old bus climbing the mountain road in the hills of Judea had to stop from time to time to cool off the engine. Next to Hannale sat an emaciated man in his forties. He had a friendly yet sad face and a thin mustache. His skin was bronzed. he smiled a few times at Hannale. At one of the frequent stops he asked her what she did. He introduced himself as Avraham Medina, the owner of a clothing store in Jerusalem. His Hebrew accent was different from the one Hannale was accustomed to. She noticed the way he pronounced the guttural "chet" and "ayin." Hannale was fascinated. When they parted in Jerusalem they decided to meet again at the bus station.

Devora and Shalom Graff lived a quiet and pleasant life in a small apartment in Jerusalem. They had immigrated to Eretz Yisrael before the war broke out from a little town in Galicia. There were overjoyed to see Hannale. Once again the floodgates of tears burst open when they heard her story. Dinner was served—chicken soup, bulbnik (potato pie), and piroges (dough, filled with onions and potatoes). The food took Hannale back to her childhood. For a moment she thought she was back home in Glinyany having dinner with her family. She told them about the young man with the beautiful skin color she had met on the bus.

"*Gevalt*, Shalom, *dus is ein frank* (woe is me, this Jew is Sephardic)."

"Yes," Shalom agreed, "most likely."

"Frank?" Hannale wondered. "What is a Frank?"

"*Oy vey*," Devora sighed as Shalom explained. "These are Jews from Mediterranean countries who lack all manners."

"A Jew is a Jew, and it doesn't matter where he is from," protested Hannale.

"I absolutely refuse to let the daughter of Aharon Hochberg see a Frank. What are we to do, Shalom?"

"Well, why don't you go with her?"

"All right," Hannale said, "but promise me you won't say anything."

"I will keep my distance, but I will accompany you wherever you go."

And so it was. When they came back, Devora covered her face with her hands and said to her husband, "Yes, a Frank."

Hannale was amused by the whole thing.

"Relax," she said. "I don't intend to see him again."

"Oh, well. Thank heaven she does credit to her family."

Hannale was interested in her courses in child psychology and development. She expected to become a teacher and educator. "Ziporah would have been proud of me if she were alive," she kept saying to herself. She felt she was continuing the tradition of her martyred sister.

When the British discovered the arms cache at *kibbutz* Yagur, the school had to move to Tel Aviv. On the bank of the Yarkon River Hannale sat and watched the green water slowly make its way to the sea. She did not have a penny to her name, but she did not mind. She was happy to live in the first Hebrew city. During one of her favorite history lessons, she was suddenly summoned to the principal's office by Masha, the secretary. Hannale was seized with a great fear. She tried hard to recall when and how she had broken any school rule.

"You are going to get very excited, Hannale," Masha said. Her heart pounded wildly as she entered Mordecai Segal's office. She saw Eju. Sudden weakness overtook her and she was about to faint. She was in shock and could not say a word. She had to sit down as she quietly whispered his name.

"Eju, my Eju, you are alive." She started to cry. Eju tried to keep calm but was unable to control himself. Tears streamed down his face. Masha burst out crying.

"Tell us about the extraordinary things that have happened to you," Mordecai Segal said, trying to relieve the mood. Hannale stood up and pressed her brother to her heart.

"Well?" Mordecai insisted.

"Yes," said Eju. "After you were shot and wounded, we received a letter from you through that German officer. If not for the intervention of Yankl Fanger's mother, he would have shot me like a dog, without hesitating. About a month later we were liberated by the Russians. Fanger killed in a battle with the Ukrainians. There was no food, and we suffered from hunger. I returned to Glinyany. Many of the Jewish homes were gone. I was told they had been burned by the Germans. I think they were dismantled and robbed by the Ukrainians. Our house was no longer there, nor was the great synagogue. As if the ground had swallowed them.

"The Pihurka family gave me some food, but we all suffered from hunger. I tried to pick apples from their tree, and when I got off the tree my boots had disappeared. I roamed the town for several days, hungry and barefooted. Finally I joined the Red Army. Now at least I had some bread and potatoes. Luckily, the political officer of the unit was a Jew, Zisha Rubin. He sent me to Berlin with a bag full of intelligence documents. When I reached Berlin I found a DP camp made up of Jewish refugees, which had been organized by the Jewish Brigade. I didn't hesitate and I deserted the Red Army. I got rid of the secret documents and discarded my uniform. The Brigade soldiers gave me a uniform of His Majesty's Army and gave me the ID papers of a member of *kibbutz* Naan who was back home at that time.

"From Berlin I was transferred to Belgium. I became friends with the Brigade members, especially a young soldier from Petah Tikva, named Yaakov Shemel, who spoke English. He was very helpful. Every time the word "payday" was heard, everyone got excited.

" 'What is "payday"?' I asked Yaakov.

" 'Don't worry,' he replied, 'I have already taken care of you.' I found out that he collected both our checks on the day the unit was paid.

"From Belgium I was transferred to Egypt. By the way, in Belgium I met Shimon, the husband of Feige from Przemyslany. He told me you were alive, that he had met you in Italy. In Egypt I got sick and I ran a high fever. I was shivering and I threw up. I was sent to a military hospital in Hilwan. I recall how I started to shake the first time I saw the black giant in a white tunic approach me with a thermometer and speak to me in a strange tongue.

"From Egypt I was smuggled into Eretz Yisrael, and I was sent to *kibbutz* Naan, where I am now."

"How did you find your sister?" Mordecai Segal asked.

"I went to the electric company in Tel Aviv and looked for the name of the Yeger family from Glinyany, which I found easily. They told me where you were."

Hannale hugged and kissed her brother and said, "Father would be proud to know we are both in the holy land."

When Hannale finished her studies in Tel Aviv she moved to Haifa and lived at the Pioneer Women House. She worked as a kindergarten teacher in Gan Yodfat. From time to time she went to visit friends at *kibbutz* Yagur. One gray morning she stood by the side of the road as thick white smoke rose from the cement factory at Nesher, and waited to hitch a ride to the *kibbutz*. A luxury car, somewhat muddy, stopped.

"I need a ride to Yagur."

"Please get in," the driver said. He was a broad-shouldered young man with a mustache, and kept smiling without saying a word.

"Are you a *sabra*?" she finally asked.

"Almost. I was born in Hungary, but I was brought here at the age of five."

"What's your name?"

"Naftali."

"A beautiful name. One of the tribes of Israel. Where are you heading for?"

"The Arab village of Jalami, where I am to meet with one of the local dignitaries."

"An Arab?" she said in surprise.

"Yes," he said, "I have many Arab friends."

"Do you speak Arabic?"

"Yes, I do."

"Aren't you afraid to go there?"

"Nonsense. I grew up with them. They themselves are great cowards. Join me and see for yourself."

She was seized by fear.

"No, thanks. I appreciate your generous offer, but I have to be at the *kibbutz*."

As he turned into the *kibbutz* she said, "No need to go in, Naftali. Drop me off near the gate. I will walk over to Hedva's hut. See, it's the one painted green."

"Good luck, be careful on the roads. What did you say your name was?"

"Hannah, Hannah Hochberg, the daughter of Aharon Hochberg."

"Hey, I didn't ask for the entire family tree. Where do you live?"

"At the Pioneer Women House in Haifa."

After he left she entered the *kibbutz* grounds through an opening in the fence. When she met Hedva, her friend noticed her excitement.

"What happened?" Hedva asked.

"This fellow, there was something about him that took my breath away."

"What fellow, what are you talking about?"

"The one who gave me a ride. I hitched a ride from Nesher. He was charming."

"He spoke three words to you and you have already decided he was charming?"

"I'm in love."

"In love? What's his name?"

"Naftali."

"Not a bad name. Good looking?"

"Gorgeous. Nearly a *sabra*."

"Where does he live?"

"I don't know. Even if I knew I wouldn't tell you. That classified information."

They both burst out laughing.

"Come," Hedva said, "I would like you to meet Avraham Shapira."

"Leave me alone," Hannale protested, "he never smiles."

"As security officer of the *kibbutz*, how do you expect him to smile? It's a very serious job."

"All right."

"Hurry up, he is waiting at the dining room."

Avraham Shapira, the busy security officer of the *kibbutz*, a senior commander of the region for the Haganah, was a short, somewhat rotund man with a serious expression.

"Aha, so this is the young woman, the kindergarten teacher who recently worked for us, the one who speaks classical Hebrew."

Hannale blushed.

"A total idiot," she thought, "this is the last time I take Hedva's advice."

"How is the young lady doing?" he asked. Hannale felt a growing repulsion.

"Get me out of here," she whispered to Hedva and pinched her hand. They chatted for a moment. Hedva said she did not feel well and they quickly left.

"Are you crazy?" Hannale said angrily.

Hedva shrugged her shoulder and gave her friend a sly smile.

"I can see the whole thing amused you. It is time for you to get to know Moshe, who works in the cowshed."

"Oh no, spare me, I may die from the smell. They say he hasn't showered since he turned twenty. How old is he now?"

"About thirty, thirty-one, something like that."

Night fell on the *kibbutz*. The wailing of the jackals was louder than usual. After a good meal at the *kibbutz* dining hall the two made their way in the scant light to the gate. The night watchman gave them cookies and hot tea. The road to the *kibbutz* was deserted. An occasional car flew by. They waited for a long time. Finally they decided to return to Hedva's room.

The next day Hannale returned to Haifa and her daily routine. In the evening she often went to the Windsor Cafe with her friends Nelly and Michael Rosenthal. One evening she saw Naftali.

"Nelly, Nelly, it's him!" Hannale said excitedly.

"Who?" Nelly asked.

"Naftali, the fellow who gave me the ride to the *kibbutz*."

Naftali was walking with a young blond woman on his arm. Her features were Slavic. Hannah got up to greet him but Nelly pulled her back to her seat.

"Don't you see he has company?"

"You are right," Hannah replied in a sad voice.

Naftali noticed her. "Small world, eh?"

"Yes," her voice trembled.

"I'd like you to meet Adina."

"Delighted," she said and extended her hand. "What a cold hand," she thought. She often always wondered about the expression "cold hand, warm heart," the opposite of which was "I have a warm hand and a warm heart."

Adina was a tall blonde. Her family were White Russians who left after the Bolshevik Revolution. Her parents had converted to Judaism and she was going to marry Naftali.

Hannale kept looking at the dancing couple. From time to time she averted her eyes when he looked back at her.

"Would you like to dance?"

The question came from a tall, thin, bespectacled man.

"No, thanks."

He turned to Nelly,

"And you?"

"Certainly," she replied.

Hannale kept thinking about Naftali. When she looked at the exit door she felt she had to leave. She got up and started towards the door. Nelly ran after her.

"Let go, I'm going home."

"If you go I go," said Nelly.

The two walked in silence. Suddenly they heard a car horn behind them. It was hard to make out the driver in the dark. The car stopped and out came Naftali. Hannah's heart beat wildly.

"Why did you run away, ladies?"

"We had to get back early," Nelly answered quickly. "Where is the lovely young woman you were with?"

"Adina? Oh, yes. She went home with Miriam. She didn't feel well. Get inside, I'll take you home."

"You don't have to," said Nelly as she entered the back seat of the car.

"So be it," Hannale mumbled, and followed her friend. When they reached the house they entered the common kitchen.

"Thanks for the ride," said Hannale.

"What's the matter," Naftali said, "don't I deserve at least a cup of coffee?"

"Of course," said Nelly, "and don't pay attention to her.

She lit the primus and gave Hannale an angry look.

"Won't she be angry if you stay?"

"Won't who be angry?"

"Your blonde. Adina is her name, I believe."

"She is no longer mine," he said and curled his mustache. A wide smile spread across his face. "My mother is against marrying a member of the Belgrad family.

"Why? She seems to be a charming person," said Nelly.

"Well, she is not exactly, not exactly. . . ."

"Not exactly what?" both of them asked.

"Not exactly suitable for our family."

"Not the right pedigree," Hannale muttered. "Was your father Graff Pototzky (a famous Polish nobleman)?"

"Excuse me?"

"Nothing," she said and blushed.

"Adina's family came to Palestine after the Russian Revolution. They were White Russians. Simple folks but kind-hearted."

"They are not Jewish?" Nelly asked. "Of course they are not," Hannale reflected. "She looks like the Greek Orthodox church on two legs."

"No, they were not originally Jewish, but they all converted."

"Why'd they do it?"

"As a gesture of solidarity with their Jewish neighbors in Nesher."

"It was good of them to do it, and it was good of their neighbors to accept them. So what is the problem, then?" Hannale asked.

"What can I say, when you get to know my mother you will understand. Adina's father is a simple bus driver from Hamovil."

"So what?"

"My mother cannot accept the idea that the son of Yozzi, the engineer who built the Nesher cement factory, would marry the daughter of a simple driver."

"There is Jewish artistocracy for you," Hannale muttered.

"Not any ordinary aristocracy," Naftali laughed. "This is Austro-Hungarian Jewish aristocracy of the Hapsburg house."

Hannale suddenly remembered her own father's adulation of this culture, and she was filled with revulsion mixed with burning hatred. She knew exactly where this enlightened culture had headed. The Third Reich was its legitimate child.

"Are you angry?" Naftali asked, somewhat apologetic.

"Not at you," she said and stroked his cheek.

"Then at whom?"

"At the Austro-Hungarian Empire."

"My mother's?"

"You won't understand. You are ninety percent *sabra*."

"What do you mean I don't understand, you don't trust. . . ." Before he had finished his sentence Hannale burst into sobs.

"Your Austro-Hungarians murdered my father and mother and sister."

"My Austro-Hungarians?"

"Naftali, I think you should leave," Nelly said and embraced Hannale.

"I'm sorry, I didn't mean. . . . Honest, I didn't. I don't give a damn about the Austro-Hungarians, they can go to hell as far as I am concerned. I'll be back, Hannah.. I swear, you will hear from me. . . this is not the end of the story. . . ."

The two women hugged each other long after he left.

"I feel terrible. I insulted him for no reason at all."

"Don't worry, he'll be back."

"Why should he come back to a hysterical woman like me?"

"He should, and how, and he knows it. I am telling you he'll be back tomorrow. Besides, you were right about the Austro-Hungarians and their pact with Germany. Austria and Germany is the same thing. They welcomed Hitler, their countryman, with great enthusiasm and outstretched arms," said Nelly.

"Pity those who are right," said Hannale. "Each time I am right I am also unlucky."

"I'm telling you, he'll be back. Let's go to sleep. It's late. The children at Gan Yodfat don't care about Austro-Hungarians or Cossak horsemen."

They slept deeply. The next day, when Hannale went back to work,

Naftali's car was parked outside the Pioneer Women House. When he saw her he blew the horn. She gave him a quick smile and went back inside. Naftali tore out of his car and ran after her.

"Shalom."

"Shalom to you."

"My name is Franz Josef."

"Delighted."

"You are invited to Windsor tonight."

"I can't go."

"Yes you can, and how. See you at 6."

She was there exactly at 6, wearing the skirt Nelly had loaned her. When he failed to appear she started to worry. She suddenly recalled his Arab friends and got scared. Finally he showed up.

"What happened?"

"Get into the car and I will tell you."

She noticed the bruise on his face.

"Are you okay?" she asked and touched him lightly.

"That bloody New Zealander will pay for it."

"Which New Zealander?"

"They had put a barrier on the road before Balad al Sheikh. Since I know most of the villagers, I was not afraid to approach it. They signaled to me to go through. When I did I saw an unfamiliar face, probably a member of one of the Arab gangs. I quickly drew my gun and started firing at them as I passed. Fortunately they scattered as soon as they heard the shots, but the fire attracted a British armored car. A New Zealander officer sat in the turret. He asked me who fired the shots. I told him it was me and he immediately ordered me to lie down on the ground. He took the gun and tried to force me into the armored car. He said, " 'An armed Jew. We will take you back to the gangs and they will take care of you.'

"I took out my Royal Air Force service card and waved it in front of his eyes.

" 'I acted in self-defense and you have no right to arrest me.'

" 'Shut up,' he barked and hit me with his rifle butt. Fortunately, at that moment Captain Simpson, who is in charge of the police station in

Nesher, came by. 'What the devil is he doing on the ground?' he asked the New Zealander lieutenant. The latter straighted up and saluted.

" 'What is going on here?' Simpson asked again.

" 'He is suspected of firing at civilians,' the lieutenant replied.

" 'Naftali, I am sorry about the incident,' Captain Simpson said, helping me up. He instructed the soldiers to take the first-aid kit out of the vehicle and take care of my wound.

"He works with us,' the captain told the New Zealander. 'He is our liaison with the Haganah. Give back his gun immediately.'

" 'I can't do it, sir, this is an illegal weapon.'

"I couldn't believe my eyes. He wrestled the gun from the New Zealander's hand and gave it to me. He wrote down the name and rank of the junior officer, addressing him harshly. He dismantled the Arab road block while muttering some graphic curses, and ordered the lieutenant to keep the traffic moving.

" 'Yes, sir,' the New Zealander said, his eyes following Naftali as if to say, 'we will meet again.'

" 'Yes, we will. And when we do, you will find out who Naftali is.' "

"First show me who Naftali is," she laughed.

"Okay, let's go, they will soon close Windsor."


"These *sabras* are like the prickly pear they are named after. Sweet inside and full of prickles on the outside," said Nelly.

"I thought he was only ninety percent *sabra* and ten percent Franz Josef."

"What's true is true."

"When are you getting married?"

"Married?" she blushed.

"You are so right for each other."

"Not so fast. I haven't even met the Baronness of the Hapsburg house."

"When will you?"

"She hasn't yet invited me to her house."

"Invite yourself if she takes her time."

"Under no circumstances."

"Well, we shall see," Nelly smiled.

"I would be interested, if possible. . .", Hannah began.

"If what is possible?" Naftali asked as they rode to Yagur on the new Harley Davidson his father had bought him.

"To meet your parents. They sound very interesting."

He turned off and started on the side road leading to Nesher.

"Where are you going?"

"You said you wanted to meet my parents."

"I am not dressed properly. I look terrible."

"It won't disturb anyone, except perhaps Tova, my sister. Don't pay any attention to her. She is somewhat ill-tempered and she has a big mouth."

"A woman has a right to have a big mouth. I'm sure she is a great beauty."

"I mean she talks too much and does not always say pleasant things to those around."

He laughed as he realized that Hannale did not quite understand native Hebrew jargon.

"Compared to my older sister Tova, my little sister Hannah is polite and civilized."

"I'm sure I'll get along with everyone."

Naftali stopped in front of the house and turned off the engine. They walked slowly towards the door. Hannale saw many cats in the yard. Two dogs were crouching on the lawn. When they saw Naftali they jumped up and wagged their tails.

"This is Pighty, and this is Vicky."

"It's a pleasure," she said.

"What did you bring us, Anty?"

Hannale heard a voice nearby. When she turned she saw a young blond woman with light blue eyes wearing a gown with the top button missing. She wore silk slippers.

"Who is this dark-haired beauty with the almond eyes?"

"Hannah Hochberg, pleased to meet you," she said and extended her hand. She almost added, "the daughter of Aharon Hochberg of Glinyany."

"Nice meeting you too, but we already have one Hannah, and I don't think we need another one."

"Shut up, Beji (Tova in Hungarian)," Naftali said. "Where are father and mother?"

"Why are you so angry at me, I'm trying to be nice to all your girlfriends. Mother is in the kitchen and father is having a meeting with Fritzi, from the Nesher board."

The house was filled with the smell of a roast; onion and paprika mixed with the smell of cigars. The living room was filled with bulky furniture and Hannale's eyes were struck by a large oil painting of puppies. There were many ashtrays filled with cigar butts. Everything seemed enchanting yet somewhat threatening.

When they entered the kitchen she saw Ilonka. She was about fifty, heavy-set, yet good-looking. Her eyes were gray-green. Her hair was in a bun, showing some gray streaks. She had a large bosom and wore a long white gown. The heat in the kitchen was unbearable, and Hannale was surprised to see that Ilonka did not sweat at all. She seemed aristocratic yet kind-hearted.

"Will you taste the food?" she asked and offered Hannale and Naftali a large wooden spoon.

"This is goulash with hot paprika." Naftali laughed when he saw Hannale sneezing and asking for water.

"She is from Galicia," he told his mother.

"Galicia? That's all right. It used to belong to us."

She recalled her father telling her about the delicacies of Vienna and Budapest. He could never eat that food because it was too spicy.

"What languages does the young lady speak?" she asked Naftali.

"Only Polish and Hebrew," he said deliberately.

"That's too bad," she said in Hungarian, "she is really lovely."

"All right, in that case she also speaks German."

"*Sprechen sie Deutsch?*"

After three hours of conversation Hannale felt she was dealing with a truly decent woman. She felt like calling her "mother," but she hesitated. Her gray-green eyes, her wisdom, her gift for listening, her tenderness, all reminded her of her own mother Rivka. The only difference was that she did not speak Yiddish. How she missed that language, rich in expressions and wise sayings, in which one could express oneself without any great effort, from "*oy vey*" and ending with "*gevalt.*" All one needed was one or two words. Compared to Yiddish, German sounded like a thin cow which gave no milk, like the mathematics she had learned in Lvov, like a wreath of thorns, like a beautiful woman with a pocked face, like goulash without paprika, like a desert without an oasis, like the clicking of SS boots. Still, she enjoyed conversing with Ilonka. She felt completely at ease with her and was willing to adopt her as her mother. With some preventive psychotherapy she would get along with Tova. Hannah arrived. She was thin and had short brown hair. She wore pants and and did not use any makeup. She had soft brown eyes and a space between her two front teeth.

"Shalom Hannah, glad to meet you."

"Glad to meet you, Hannale."

"Hannale is short for Hannah."

"Right. Well, where are you from?"

"Yagur. At the moment I live at the Pioneer Women House in Haifa."

"What do you do?"

"I am a teacher at the kindergarten in Yodfat."

"I work for the Jewish Agency."

"Very important work," said Hannale. "They gave me the certificate to come here. Do you know Ben-Gurion and Sharret?"

"Yes, I meet with them frequently."

"Really? What do you think of our chances to have our own state?"

"Very good, if the Revisionists stop the terrorism."

"Hannah was an officer in the British Army," Naftali said.

"What is all this noise about?" Tova interrupted. "By the way, did Peter call?"

"Pardon me, who is Peter?"

"He is not yet part of the family so I can't tell you."

"Be quiet," Naftali said. "Peter is her British friend. I met him at the harbor. He told me his parents are against him marrying a Jew."

"You bastard, I'll show you. The first chance I get I'm becoming Christian. Actually not, the Catholics are garbage. The best is no religion at all and none of this nonsense."

"The best thing is Spiritualism," Naftali snickered.

"Poor thing," Ilonka fumed. "Again he hasn't called."

"Perhaps he can't marry you for reasons of religion and conscience," Naftali went on. Hannale put her hand on his mouth.

"He means no harm. I'm sure he'll call you. Do you go to school?"

"She was kicked out of school."

"That's enough, Naftali. What do you do?"

"I am a dental assistant."

"And you make a good salary. It's time you started sharing the household expenses."

"It's time to go," Hannale said. "I was happy to meet all of you."

On the way out they ran into Yozzi.

"Hello, father."

"Hello, Anty. What are you doing at home? You were supposed to be at the harbor."

"Please meet my friend Hannah."

Hannale noticed the great respect with which Naftali addressed his father. Yozzi was a tall man with a tanned face, clear eyes and a high forehead. He had a square jaw with a cigar stuck in the corner of his mouth. He was dressed in kakhi. He was obviously was very strong. He wore a safari hat and looked like an English gentleman.

"She speaks German, Dad."

Yozzi nodded and went inside. When they mounted the motorcycle they heard loud voices in Hugarian.

"She is being rude to him again."

"Who?"

"Tova, who else?"

"Why?"

"It's about money."

"What does she do with the money?"

"She buys clothes and makeup."

"It's her right."

"You defend everybody."

"She is your sister. You should do the same."

"She hates me."

"Impossible."

"Wait and see. Besides, I introduced you to my father as my girlfriend."

"Really."

"Yes. Is it true?"

"Get going. We were supposed to be in Yagur 6 hours ago."

When they walked down the path to the dining hall she asked, "Why did you mention Spiritualism before?"

"You promise you won't tell?"

"You were serious?"

"Well, it's a little hard to talk about, but. . . how should I put it, my mother and my sister are Spiritualists, or something like that."

"What exactly is it?"

"Believe it or not, I don't know exactly. It is something like the witch of En Dor in the Biblical stories of King Saul. It has to do with communicating with the dead, I am not sure how it's done."

"They do it at home?"

"No. A few times a month they go to Bat Galim, where the chief 'Witch of En Dor,' Hermina, lives."

"The chief?"

"Yes. They say they can talk through her to the dead. I'm confused by this whole thing. But my father has nothing to do with all this nonsense."

"But they do seem to be good women, especially your mother."

"Yes, she is a good person, and she loves me very much."

"So let's forget the whole thing."

"I've already told you, you are everyone's friend. Tell me, do you think every person has a good side to them?"

"Not, not at all. Some people are pure evil."

"It's strange how you say it with such certainty."

"They exist, and how," said Hannale, and her cheeks became moist. Whenever she cried Naftali felt uneasy, as if he had done something wrong. He knew a horrible story hid behind this warm and pleasant face. He was afraid to ask, yet he felt an obligation to find out about her past. The survivors of the Nazi hell had brought many stories with them, and occasionally he would hear one. Each story made him grit his teeth with fury. He would mutter under his breath, "Those bastards, those stinking Ukrainians, I would shoot them without a trial and without mercy". He knew about the concentration camps and the gas chambers. He would never understand how they could have gone like sheep to the slaughter and why they had never defended themselves. Where was the Haganah, or even the Irgun, and the LEHI? Why didn't they organize? Sometimes he pictured himself being led to slaughter, snatching a German's weapon and killing him and his buddies, exacting sweet revenge, then being lifted on his fellow Jews' shoulders and proclaimed a hero as they all start singing and dancing. He wanted things to have turned out differently. He wished to be proud of his fellow Jews, but he couldn't. Hannale detected a look of despair in his eyes, changing to sadness.

"You must wonder why I cry so much?"

"I know," he said. "You were in a death camp and you saw your parents going to take a shower and not returning. I know everything about the gas chambers."

"Gas chambers? Why gas chambers? First, my parents were killed by the Ukrainians, and second, I was in a labor camp and I escaped and became a partisan."

"A Jewish partisan? Impossible. What are you talking about? Did you have weapons?"

"Yes, the boys and I had weapons in the forest."

"What forest and what weapons? You mean to tell me you fired at the Germans?"

She burst into a laughter.

"We fired in the direction of the Germans, yes, we did. And how do you like planned raids on German army convoys? Or raids on Polish and Ukrainian homes to liquidate antisemites and murderers of Jews?"

"God Almighty! There were people like this? All I was told was that it was like the slaughterhouse of Kfar Hasidim (a small village in the Haifa area). Damn it, you have no idea how I feel. I feel as though I have been born again. What can I say, I'm so happy to hear this."

"It's midnight, let's go home."

"Home to the Pioneer Women house?"

"Yes."

"Aren't you cold?"

"No."

"Take my jacket."

"No, thanks. I'm always warm. Even when it snowed in the forest I wasn't cold. The heat in this country is killing me."

"It won't snow here for a long time."

"I don't miss the snow."

"I believe you." He started racing towards Haifa, and he could feel her heartbeat as she clung to him from behind.

"Are you afraid we may turn over or are you afraid of me?"

"A little of this and a lot of the other."

"How did you survive all this?" he asked, his curiosity mounting.

"You know, even in this evil Sodom and Gomorrah there were a few righteous people."

"What do you mean?" he asked.

"Walter, Dr, Mutie and that medic, what was his name? Damn it. My mind is blocked. Laurence. That's it. I wish I could find them and talk to them. I want to tell them that. . . . I don't know what I'm going to say when I see them. What have you heard about the German army?"

"What everybody knows about the Nazi bastards. When we finally defeated them in the Western Desert I was assigned to guard them in a P.O.W. camp. When one of them noticed my Palestine tag, he asked, 'Yuden?' I nodded yes, and he arrogantly drew his finger across his neck. I lost control. If it weren't for my fellow soldiers, who dragged me away, that guy would not have lived another minute. Who are the people you mentioned before?"

"Look here," she said, as she lifted her shirt and raised her left arm. "What do you see?"

"It looks like two small round scars, almost like bullet scars. My god, were you shot?"

"Yes, I was machine-gunned after a German raid on us."

"But no one survives such a wound; wasn't it next to your heart and lungs"

"Right again," she said. "My lungs collapsed. Who do you think saved my life?"

"Not one of them," he replied. "It can't be."

As she nodded, he whispered, "You mean to say that these three individuals—these Germans—saved your life? They didn't know you were Jewish, did they?"

She nodded again.

"Unbelievable, unbelievable," he mumbled. "Were they in the Wehrmacht?"

"First Tank Division retreating from Russia. A doctor, a medic and an intelligence officer."

"We must find them. After we get married we'll go to Germany to look for them."

"You really mean it?" she asked, weeping again.

"About the wedding, or about finding them?" he chuckled.

"It's midnight. Let's go home."

"I don't believe her son would marry a Galician girl. After all, they are a respectable family."

The speaker was Mrs. Lipsky, who ran into Ilonka at the Nesher commissary.

"Give me some more of that Hugarian sausage, Diussi."

"What did she say?" Ilonka asked the Transylvanian grocer.

"I'd rather not mix in," he answered in Hungarian. "It's not my business. You know my Hebrew is not too good. She said something about Galicia."

"Yes, it must be about my daughter-in-law to be."

"She doesn't think she is suitable for your family."

"You filth," Ilonka snapped at the woman and switched back to Hungarian.

"It bothers her because the young woman happens to be a real catch, a thousand times better than her Judith the little gossip-monger."

The grocer turned pale when asked to translate Ilonka's words. He quickly calculated that Mrs. Praff bought three times as much as Mrs. Lipsky.

"I only want to warn you against the Galicians," Yemima Lipsky said and left the store looking offended, which she may or may not have been.

"Diusi, if you hear anyone say anything bad about the wedding, let me know."

"Sure, Mrs. Praff, you can trust me."

Rabbi Kaniel, the respected rabbi of Haifa, whose long white beard made him look distinguished, wanted to know exactly what Hannale had been through. He kept nodding without saying a word. When she finished he told her she had to immerse herself in the ritual bath before the wedding.

Hannale was somewhat offended. "Is this all he has to say to me?"

Eju came to the wedding from the *kibbutz* with mud on his boots. It was hard for him to get rid of the cowshed smell that clung to them. He was asked many questions about the *kibbutz*, about his work in the dairy and his wish to become a driver. He said that his parents and sister had perished in the Holocaust, and he had an older brother who might be living in Russia. He escaped before the Germans reached Glinyany. Where was Glinyany? In Galicia. Yes, we are Galicians. We don't look like Galicians? How do Galicians look? No, I am not married. He was also asked about Hannale. She is a teacher for preschoolers. No, it's not a good enough trade. She is very capable. Why has she replaced Adina? Who is Adina? I really don't know. She is the one in the corner. She is very cute. What is it like to live on a *kibbutz*? A lot of work? Where is the *kibbutz*? Near Jerusalem. Yes, there are problems with the Arabs in Bab El Wad. We are holding our own. You ask if we belong to Hashomer Hatzair? No, we belong to Achdut Ha'avoda and Mapai (more to the center of the political range). No, we are not communists. There are about 120 members in the *kibbutz*. The weather? Yes, sometimes I drink fresh milk. No, I don't work in the fields, I work with the cows. Straight from the cow. Yes, it tastes good. I am two years younger than Hannale. Yes, I also speak German, Polish, Yiddish, and Ukrainian. That's true, a German saved her life. It's hard to believe there are good Germans. Where is he? We don't know. There was also a doctor; we can't locate him either. Incredible stories. Yes, you can visit the *kibbutz*, the children may enjoy it. Yes, it's true, we eat together in the dining hall and take turns in the kitchen. You can eat there too. See you. All the best. No, no, there is no sleeping around.

"Are you enjoying yourself? Hannale asked."

"No, I am not. All the time *Egan, Teshik, Egan, Teshik* (yes, please, in Hungarian). These people want to know everything."

"Oh god, Eju, where are they?" She forgot all about them. Where was her father. Wasn't he supposed to give her away? He would love to chat in German with all these Hapsburg descendants. And where the hell was her mother? Wasn't she supposed to shed tears of joy around the *Huppa* (Jewish matrimonial canopy)? Was Munyu so busy with his friends at the Zionist club that he forgot to come? And Ziporah? Couldn't she take the time from her teaching to share her sister's *Simcha* (a joyful event)?

"Where are they, Eju? Can't you tell me? Where is Walter, and Dr. Mutie, and Laurence, and Yulka, and Michelle, and Herr Kozzi, and Doctor Singer? Why aren't they here?"

"They are here in your heart, all of them. Hannale, I feel so far away from these Huns and Madiars (the tribes from which the Hungarians are believed to be descendants)."

"Stop. Go eat something." she ordered him as she calmed down.

"I'm bursting."

"It's lucky the rabbi insisted on the food being kosher. Otherwise they would be wolfing tons of Hungarian sausage." she giggled.

Unfortunately, the Galician side was poorly represented. Devora and Shalom Graff, and the Yeger and Buchbinder families, and Eju, of course, but no one else was there. The rest were a mixture of Austro-Hungarians. Hagana members (the Jewish self-defense organization), Israel Nesher residents, English officers and Arab and Druse sheiks, not to forget the spiritualists.

"Well, well, if our parents saw you in your wedding dress getting married to a Hapsburg nobleman, they would be ecstatic."

"Stop it. Start behaving. They are nice people."

"I'm getting a headache from the Hungarian. Let's talk a little in Yiddish."

"Are you crazy? Not now. They asked me if you could bring them some milk power from the *kibbutz*?"

"They weren't ashamed, eh?"

"The father is shameless. Look over there, see the tall Englishman with the hat?"

"What is he, a policeman?"

"No, he is Tova's boyfriend. She is dying for him to marry her and take her to England. She has a complex about being Jewish."

"A little bit of Hitler wouldn't be bad for her, she might wake up and remember who she is."

"What's true is true, but that's not her luck."

"Peter, meet my brother, Eju. Here we call him Yehudah."

"How do you do, Judah? It's a Biblical name, isn't it?"

"How do you do?"

"This is it. I've had it. I'm going back to Glinyany. I don't belong here."

"To whom in Glinyany? Zenig Tuss? You don't belong there. You belong here. Father would be proud to know we have finally arrived here."

"I've had it with all of your Hungarians and Hapsburgs and Englishmen. I'd like to get back to my cows."

"You'll have to get used to it and come more often."

The wedding was joyous and elegant. There was no wild dancing, only tangos and waltzes. The Praff family moved to the German colony, not far from the the Haifa harbor. It was a charming house, built of stone, a red-tiled roof. In the back was a fruit orchard and a small yard. The neighbors were pleasant and the neighborhood, built at the turn of the century by German Templars who had landed in Palestine, was quiet and safe.

The young couple moved into the Praff's former wood-frame house in Nesher. Naftali joined the new Israel Defense Forces and became a sergeant major. Because of his experience with organization and equipment he was detailed to a logistics unit. Hannale became an experienced homemaker. When she got up in the morning she thought she was in Glinyany. Sometimes she imagined she was Rivka Hochberg, sitting on her doorstep. She put on some weight.

Those were the early days of the new State of Israel. Each morning, when she woke up, she felt a miracle had happened to her. Sometimes she was in Nesher and sometimes in Glinyany. It was all the same. Her father would look down at her from heaven and say, "This is what I taught you, Hannale. I am so proud of you. Once in a while her mother would visit. "This is how you make Bulbnik? This is gefilte fish?" Rivka would chide.

Two years later she had her first child, a girl named Ronit. Her Jewish name was Rivka, but it was made Hebrew so as not to remind one of the former life, yet perpetuate her mother's memory. The girl was pretty, but a devil.

"Let her cry," Ilonka would say sternly. "Why are you holding her so long? Don't change her diaper until she becomes toilet-trained."

"*Oy vey zmir mamaleh vos ken ich machen* (dear mother, what can I do)?"

She continued to change the diaper and held Ronit in her arms to prevent her from crying.

"Overprotective," her neighbor from across the street, Nafusi, decided. "Look at my Avena, running loose around the village since the age of one, not afraid of anything."

She often checked Freud's writings and the *kibbutz* literature on child development and but did not find any answers to her questions. "Well, I guess I'll have to trust my own instincts. *Nu, vus zugst mameh* (what do you say, mother)?"

Naftali was the happiest man in Nesher. He held his daughter longer than his wife and took her with him everywhere in the village. The next child was cirumcised. Dr. Zeitlin, the affable village doctor, had teased Naftali that the next child would be circumcised. And so it was. The next child was yours truly, Dr. Giora Aharon Praff, who is now writing these lines. After me came Nadav, and I was somewhat forgotten, since Nadav was mother's baby.

## *Epilogue*

As you have probably figured out, my mother was a remarkable woman. I am sure you are curious about the rest of her life. Well, it wasn't a smooth ride at all—almost like the story so far.

After all the wandering and adventures you have read about so far came the routine anxieties of an ordinary mother who raised her children in the Land of Israel. She never had a calm day since the birth of her children.

She devoted her entire life to educating and caring for mentally retarded children, and supporting their families. She received numerous awards and great recognition for her important and dedicated work.

She made a great effort to locate Walter Rosenkranz, who was stranded in the east part of Germany after the war. You can imagine their meeting in East Berlin when she was allowed by the communist authorities to make a one-day trip to this once-divided city. This wonderful man, a German Righteous of Nations, may have been just one of many human beings whose stories will remain forever unknown. These Germans took an immense risk in helping her. This story is about Walter and other Righteous of Nations in Sodom and Gomorrah.

My mother instilled in me a love for Israel, as well as many other values which are psychological and emotional. I have devoted my life to medicine and helping others with the kind of feelings and compassion she taught me.

I absorbed her personal history as I sat on her knee as a tiny tot. May God be my witness. How I imagined spening night after night hiding in a bunker in the woods of Mount Carmel while the Germans were looking for me. I would hear her ask our Arab maid if she would hide her and the family at her house in case Israel ceased to exist.

I nurtured these fears, but I also inherited the pride of someone able to hold out her arms as she encouraged me during some desperate moments in my military service. She read most of this book before she died and my heart was filled with joy when I visited Glyniany, Lvov, Jachtorow and Korwicze and told her about my trip.

When I sat at her deathbed, she made me swear to carry on the memory of her family and the story of her people to my children and others. She may or may not have realized how much I wanted to fulfill her desire and how intense my feelings were all those years. She surveyed my work and assured me that I had captured it all.

I have much more to say to you, wondrous mother, but I can't go on. My thoughts are no longer clear, and I'm beginning to choke on my tears.

The author's mother, Israel 1947.